SKIPPING

SCHOOL

SKIPPING

SCHOOL

Jessie Haas

GREENWILLOW BOOKS, New York

Library of Congress Cataloging-in-Publication Data

Haas, Jessie.
Skipping school / by Jessie Haas.
p.   cm.
Summary: Fifteen-year-old Phillip feels isolated
and confused as he tries to cope with his father's
terminal illness and his family's recent move from
their farm to a home in the suburbs.
ISBN 0-688-10179-8
[1. Family life—Fiction.   2. Schools—Fiction.
3. Sick—Fiction.   4. Moving, Household—Fiction.]
I. Title.   PZK.H1129Sk 1992   [Fic]—dc20
91-37642   CIP   AC

FOR WILLY—

SUPERVISOR, BEST FRIEND

S K I P P I N G

S C H O O L

CHAPTER ONE

It was time for the captains to choose their teams:
the soccer field, gym class, ten o'clock in the morning. The sun had not yet peered over the rim of the
bowl of land that surrounded the Union High School,
and the grass was white with frost.

Phillip waited while the best players were snapped up
around him. People were encouraging their teeth to
chatter or blowing out their breath in big white clouds.
Goose bumps chased across Phillip's arms. His legs
took on a purple cast, and his windpipe burned from the
laps he'd run. The cold was the first thing that had
made him feel alive all morning.

"Johnson," said a voice: Kris's hotshot brother Greg.
He moved over to that group, putting on a yellow vest.

"You're left fullback," Greg told him, in a neutral voice, refusing to acknowledge even in tone that Phillip was his sister's friend and someone he saw fairly often in his own home.

Phillip jogged slowly back to position. At his old school he'd usually played fullback, too . . . .

It was a mistake to recall that. In the blank seconds before the game began, he could not squeeze back the memories: hot midwestern autumn games, his friend Rob the goalie behind him, corn rustling in the field nearby, and after school, five hundred hogs to feed . . . his father's cough. The auction.

The whistle ripped away the memories. The other team had plenty of hotshots, too. When they got the ball through, Phillip stopped it, with his thighs, with his back. Once he bounced it off his head. When he couldn't touch the ball, he blocked, unflinchingly. And he ignored the praise bestowed on him by Greg: "Good boy, Phil!" "Nice save!" The man was a politician. In the halls he and Phillip passed without a word, and Phillip didn't see why he should speak now.

The yellow vests won. Phillip limped from the field, bearing a red ball mark, a grass-stained graze, a few bruises. Into the locker room, into the hot, hot shower beating the cold and ache out of his bones.

"Okay, everybody out!" The coach glanced into the shower. "Johnson!"

Phillip turned off the shower, dried and slowly dressed himself. The bell rang. People left, people came in, and he wondered if he could stay, put on his shorts, go out and play another game. . . .

"Johnson! Out!"

He picked up his books and went out the locker-room door. Straight ahead of him, down a long orange-carpeted hall, the sun shone through the double glass front doors.

Dust motes filtered down through the sunbeams. Outside, across acres of green lawn and playing fields, wind shook and loosened the autumn leaves. The maples were bare now. Only the beeches and the sad-colored oaks were left. The sky was brilliant above them.

People who left early, to go to jobs or home to babies, went out the doors. Mr. Pilewski, the attendance monitor, watched with half an eye as he talked to the janitor.

A stream of sweet air stirred in the stagnant hallway, drawing Phillip irresistibly. The door was just closing behind the last person. He caught it and went through. A gust of wind blew on his wet hair, as if he'd just dunked his head in ice water.

He walked purposefully toward the far side of the parking lot. No one called after him. He was so new that few students knew his name. He had never caused trouble before.

Reaching the last line of cars, he turned and looked back. People were driving away with a lot of tire-squealing and bad-muffler noises. A small teacherlike figure opened the big door and looked out. Slowly a few people sitting on the benches got up and went inside. Then there was no one in sight.

Phillip turned and scrambled up the bank into the trees, gained the top of the ridge, and went over the other side.

The woods were laced with trails used by the cross-country runners. During the first eight weeks of gym his class had run over these trails, and this gave Phillip a useful knowledge now. Easily and swiftly he followed the worn paths, and after a few minutes came out on a dirt road.

Here the gym class turned left, reentered the woods a hundred yards downhill, and returned by artificially winding routes to the school. Phillip turned right and walked briskly uphill, feeling steadily more matter-of-fact and cheerful.

It was ironic, he thought—or disgusting, or ridiculous, some such word—that he, a farm boy who now lived in a suburban-looking development at the edge of town, should be bused out into the country to the Union High School. Here was everything he longed for: the silent woods, the road less and less used as he walked along it, until grass started growing up between the tracks, and, over the next hill, a farm.

It occupied a whole valley, vast by New England standards, the autumn grass yellow-green in the marshy, hummocked pastures. The earth of the cornfields was rich and black, combed with rows of pale gold stubble. Here and there along the rusty fence lines an extra post, rotted at the bottom, seemed to float on the wire purely for decoration. Phillip could smell cow manure and silage, a combination like overripe cheddar.

As he watched, a tractor left the barnyard, pulling a full manure spreader. It headed out to the cornfield, and soon the manure was flying up behind. Big Holstein cows ambled out the barn door, with a heavy, footsore gait. They stood looking glumly at their watery pasture. Someone walked across the yard toward the house, followed by a collie dog.

The cold wind blew tears into Phillip's eyes. He looked a moment more at the long red barn, the yellow house with the frost-nipped geraniums in the window boxes. Then he turned away. He couldn't go down there. He was a truant, an outlaw.

He turned uphill, trying not to be disappointed at the emptiness and quiet of the woods.

After a few minutes he began to notice sounds: jays; a far-off crow; the silly bark of the collie; chickadees; chipmunks.

A brook.

It was below the road, and he walked down to it. A foot wide and three inches deep, it gushed merrily over miniature rapids. Phillip put in his hand and drew it out ice cold. He scooped a palmful of water to his mouth. It tasted sweet and clean.

He climbed back up to the road and continued walking. He really wondered, now, just what the hell he was doing.

But the road led upward, and he followed, quoting to himself from Tolkien:

> The Road goes ever on and on,
> Down from the door where it began.
> Now far away the Road has gone. . . .

This road went on around a corner, and there was a house.

CHAPTER TWO

A small gray-shingled house with flaking white trim, it was set off the road near the brook. Black locust trees ringed it, their huge trunks dark and deeply fissured, the bare branches straggling wild across the sky. Before the stone doorstep the grass grew rank, and there was patch of sand. The rags of a very old towel hung on a limp clothesline.

The house was so gray, so quiet and abandoned, that Phillip at first thought nothing of it. He stopped and looked, but then he very nearly walked on. Only as he took the first step did he remember his dream. Last night? Last week? . . .

A black night, wild and rainy. Someone riding hard up a dangerous road, full of enemies, coming to a house by a brook. He knocks, and someone answers the door. Watching from outside, behind the rider, in the rain, Phillip sees that the person coming to the door with a candle is himself. A message is passed. They both look up the stormy black road, full of enemies and defeat.

Is the rider taken in? Or does the man with the candle dress himself and go forth? Phillip could not remember, but he felt the blackness around him and the rain on his skin, saw the lightning, saw the house, the stone doorstep, the grass and patch of sand ... real sand, dream sand, slightly separated as when you cross your eyes. ...

He squeezed his eyes shut, but when he opened them, the house was still there. Perhaps it was not quite the same. Perhaps the dream house had been smaller, perhaps the brook not quite so near. He had seen it only in the dark, after all.

He went down through the grass, skirting the patch of sand, mounted the doorstep, and knocked.

He could tell immediately that the house was empty, and that was a relief. He had not believed that the door would be opened, that he would face himself standing there holding a candle. But now the chill on his skin was just the chill of early November and no jacket. The house was empty, and when he pushed down the thumb latch, the door opened.

He looked into a dusty room, with plaster, leaves, and dry raccoon dung on the floor. A huge stone fireplace faced him, square in front of the door. To the left he could see another doorway, another room.

He stepped gingerly across the floor. One or two places felt soft, but nothing actually gave way. There were rustling sounds: mice beneath the floorboards and the leaf piles in the corners. Spider webs hung in dusty tatters from the ceiling. No spiders in sight; their brief seasonal lives were already finished. Future spiders hung in soft brown egg cases in the webs.

The back room was in even worse shape. The floor

sloped sharply downhill. Some of the boards were broken, the holes filled with leaves that had blown through the door, which hung open on one hinge.

It had been the kitchen. A filthy soapstone sink stood against the back wall, and at one end of it a hand pump was mounted. An unpainted square of floor showed where the gas range had stood, and there was another for the refrigerator. But there was nothing left except the sinkful of leaves, rustling apprehensively as Phillip approached.

He tried to move cautiously, but the slope of the floor hurried him, and his foot broke through a rotten board. A musty, decaying smell arose, most unpleasantly.

From the back door he looked out on the brook.

It flowed not ten feet from the doorstep, more slowly here, for the ground flattened and a few large rocks formed a dam. The water was so clear that Phillip could see the softly rounded green stones on the bottom. Near the brook was an aluminum kettle. When he walked down to look, he saw that the bottom was rusted out.

He drank again, and something like happiness shot painfully through his chest as his lips touched the water. He shoved his face under the surface. The water gushed through the roots of his hair, cold and fresh. He wanted to breathe it, almost couldn't stop himself, had to come up and gulp the cold clear air instead.

"Wow!" He shook his head, and the drips flew.

Sitting back on his heels, he looked around the hollow. Its dreariness suited him so exactly—the snaggling black branches; the tall brown grasses and the seed-pods rattling in the wind—that he was filled with exultance. This place was meant for him, and he had found it.

Urgently, now, something was pushing him—something to be done! The need buzzed along the insides of his arms and the backs of his legs. But what?

His eye fell on a branch, blown into the corner of the step. Good kindling: He broke it into fireplace lengths over his leg. The yard was littered with sticks of all sizes, and he began to gather them.

The thin ones he could break to a useful length, but the good pieces that would sustain a fire, he could only pile. To accomplish anything more, he needed a chain saw—or better, given his secret presence here, an ax. After many trips he had a large pile of what was essentially kindling.

It didn't matter. He had no matches, and he wasn't going to embarrass himself by squatting on the hearth, rubbing two dry sticks together. But he felt good, looking at his pile of limb wood.

Still, it was a pitiful harvest by the old standard. He remembered the drive across the cold cornfields from the woodlot, truck full of logs, his ears droning from a day of chain saw noise. Afternoons at the hydraulic splitter, afternoons stacking till the shed was full, and then stacking next year's wood outdoors on pallets.

Come to think of it, the wood meant for this winter must still be out there. He wished he could get it. . . .

But the new people had probably stacked it in the

shed to burn. Probably the pallets were already full of wood for next winter. It never ended. He remembered his dismay when he had first realized this. All the autumns of his life had stretched before him, blasted with the roar of chain saws, gritty with sawdust and wood dirt.

No more. Now they lived in a house that took care of itself. Its vinyl clapboards never needed painting, and heat ran automatically through the baseboard heaters. It had wall-to-wall carpet and picture windows that looked out at other picture windows, other vinyl siding.

This is better, he thought, looking around the bare, dirty room, with the big pile of kindling and the wind blowing through.

But for now he had to leave.

□   □   □

When he came over the bluff, the buses waited empty in the schoolyard.

Phillip came down the slope in a low, swift scramble, landing on his knees in front of somebody's car, straightened, and walked innocently and forthrightly across the parking lot. No one was in sight.

Very faintly, now, he heard the bell ringing. As he approached, people began pouring out the doors. He joined, unnoticed, and boarded his own bus.

It was Kris who brought him back to earth. Kris, the first and the only friend he'd made here. He hadn't given her a thought all day, but she'd obviously thought about him.

"Where *were* you?" She sounded both anxious and angry, and her glittering blue eyes seemed to pierce him through.

Phillip could only gape. He hadn't wasted a moment in thinking up a story. He couldn't begin to think of one now.

Kris frowned at him. Her pale brows were nearly invisible, but he could see the swirl of muscle. "Were you sick? Were you in the nurse's office?"

That would be a possible story, Phillip realized. But too late: He was already shaking his head in a nerveless way. Kris flushed, and looked down at the books on her lap. They'd only known each other for three months. That was too soon for accountability, but it was definitely soon enough for discomfort.

Suddenly Phillip noticed the crumpled lunch bag on the seat between them.

"Do you have food left?"

"My apple."

"Can I have it? I missed lunch."

Kris looked him over: no books, no homework, no jacket. She nodded.

Phillip tore the apple out of the bag and struck his teeth into it. The white flesh melted before his hunger like spring snow. About as filling, too.

Nibbling daintily around the hard seedcases, he glanced across to see Kris watching him. Older, he thought instantly. It was the question that he'd been answering ever since he first met her: Is she older than me, or younger? They were in the same class, but that didn't mean much.

"What happened in English?" he asked, trying to retrieve a sense of normality. Then he wished he'd said something different, or else kept his mouth shut.

Kris's voice was smooth and cool. "More speeches. We learned how to do a manicure. . . ."

"Sorry I missed that!" said Phillip brazenly. Kris didn't give him the satisfaction of so much as a glance.

"Then Lester McCoy taught us how to run a trap line, and Angela Vasco painted a masterpiece before our very eyes." Slight pause. "Have you written *your* speech yet?" She knew he hadn't—Phillip could tell from her voice.

He shook his head. Not only had he not written it; he didn't even have a topic. "Something you know how to do," the teacher had said. "Something you think other people would find interesting, and something of reasonable size to bring to class." The teacher was young and bright-eyed and optimistic. Phillip felt older than she was sometimes. Kris was definitely older.

Kris glanced sidelong at him. She was a student of animal behavior, and Phillip felt as if he'd suddenly turned into a laboratory rat, one that persisted in running the maze backward. All her powers of observation were trained on him. "You're next on the list," she said in a cool, experimental tone. "For tomorrow morning."

Something you know how to do, thought Phillip desperately. Reasonable size. Nothing he knew how to do was a reasonable size: driving a combine, chopping corn, running a wood splitter. . . .*Wood! Ax!*

"I'll do a wood splitting demonstration," he said to Kris, with what he could not help but feel was superb casualness. "Do you think your father would drive me in tomorrow?" Kris's father was a much-dreaded biology teacher here at the high school.

"I'll tell him," said Kris. She gave him another assessing once-over, not as impressed as Phillip had hoped, settled deeper into the corner of the seat, and opened a book. She hardly ever did that on the bus, and Phillip knew exactly how to take it.

CHAPTER THREE

The bus let him out at the veterinarian's clinic where he worked. Phillip got off with a sense of relief and stood for a moment watching as the bus lumbered away up the busy commercial strip. Kris wasn't a waver, but she especially didn't wave today. Phillip tried to shrug off a feeling of apprehension as he let himself through the side-door into the office.

Dr. Rossi sat at her desk, small, elegant, and poised, balancing her pencil on its tip and looking up at Dr. Franklin. He was shouting.

"Of course I can take one! Hell—I can take 'em all! I've only got seven cats and three dogs, and who needs to get married and start a family? Mother Teresa didn't, and look at her!"

Phillip looked more closely, and saw that what he'd taken for a black doctor's bag in Dr. Franklin's hand was actually a small cat carrier. The open end was toward Phillip, and he had only to bend slightly at the knees to see inside.

One of the kittens. Of course.

"Hugh . . ." said Dr. Rossi, sounding tentative but compelled. "Hugh, you're tearing yourself to pieces over this."

"I'd like to tear something to pieces! My God . . . the miracle of birth! Can you believe it? That's what the silly bitch actually said to me when she brought them in. 'I wanted the kids to see the miracle of birth.' And then she's ready to flush the little bastards down the toilet!"

"Yes, Hugh, reprehensible. But—if I could just advise you—you'll be dealing with this for the next thirty years. You can't afford to get so personally involved—"

"I'm not sure I can afford the thirty years! My God . . . the greyhounds are bad enough. But at least they get some life! They get a few years before they're used up and thrown away. But—"

Dr. Rossi's sad eyes strayed past him. "Oh. Hello, Phillip."

"Hi," said Phillip. "Cages?"

"Yes," said Dr. Rossi.

Phillip was the peon here, the one who did the dirtiest jobs, physically and morally: from cleaning litter boxes to restraining animals for killing, from sweeping and mopping to stoking the incinerator with trash and sometimes bodies. On good days he loved his job, days when no greyhounds from the local racetrack had to be killed simply because they weren't fast enough; when there were no abandonments; when the tragedies were simple, natural, sometimes fixable. Phillip was interested in fixable tragedies.

The dog cages were empty today. No greyhounds.

But the cat cages were full. He got the garbage pail and started to empty litter boxes. In the office Dr. Franklin spoke again, more quietly.

"Madeline. Couldn't you . . ."

"No," said Dr. Rossi gently. "I can't keep them past tomorrow. There's always another litter coming, and you know I can't keep them all."

"But what are we doing to ourselves? Can we just keep killing all these animals? It's not even to end suffering! It's just throwing them away! Can we keep on doing this for thirty years and not turn into monsters?"

Dr. Rossi's voice dropped to a murmur.

"I know he's in the next room! He's not a child! He's got the same questions I do!"

"Well, for God's sake don't ask *me!*" cried Dr. Rossi. "*I* don't know!"

"But you go ahead and do it anyway?"

"Yes, Hugh, yes! And so do you, and so does Phillip!

And I go home and cry about it—but you won't make me cry here and now! I've got work to do!" Phillip heard the chair scrape back, and a moment later the door to the waiting room banged shut.

Dr. Franklin came through the back room, cat carrier in hand. His beard was on his chest, his gray eyes wide and thoughtful. He glanced down the row of cat cages and saw Phillip. After a moment's pause he set the carrier down and went to the last cage, where the litter of kittens had been living for two weeks now. There were three left: little tigers, fat and healthy. Dr. Franklin took them out and managed to cuddle all three against his bearded face.

"Any chance you can take one of these guys, Phil?"

"No," said Phillip. "I—things are situated so I can't."

"That's right," said Dr. Franklin. "I remember—you saved a greyhound once, didn't you, and you gave it away."

"Yeah." That was Diana, and he'd given her to Kris.

Dr. Franklin shook his head, an unwise move which waggled his beard enticingly. The kittens' eyes brightened, and they pounced, heedless of their precarious positions almost six feet in the air.

"Ow!" Dr. Franklin tried to retract his chin. The beard wiggled. Pounce!

"Oh, shit," Dr. Franklin said suddenly. He dumped the kittens back in their cage and turned away from them. "Bye, Phil." The door banged shut behind him.

"Phillip?" Dr. Rossi looked through the doorway behind him. "Can you help me with a dog?"

"Just a second. I have to fill the litter boxes."

"Hurry. The life you save will probably be mine!"

The patient was a large, woolly Airedale with a wound on its hip. Phillip's job was to hold the dog's front end after Dr. Rossi had tied its jaws shut with an old nylon, a fancy black stocking with pearly glitters and a seam up the back. Above it the dog's eyes were sullenly narrow. A growl vibrated in its chest throughout the examination.

"He hates you," Phillip said.

"And he's getting to know my scent awfully well," said Dr. Rossi. "I should have thought to use someone else's stocking."

"I can think of a few people," said his owner, laughing. "I'll bring you a supply next time!"

Finished with the dog, Phillip returned to the silent room. The laughter, a black, spangled stocking with a seam up the back, the round-limbed bounce and violence of the Airedale were gay and colorful in his head. The blank room with its cream-colored cement walls and big bank of cages seemed to swallow all that. He measured out the cat food, and its dry rattle in the dishes, the can opener, were the only sounds.

But as the heavy scent of cat food rose from the opened cans, cries came from the last cage. A short, fat kitten paw reached out through the grid and groped around blindly. Phillip found himself laughing.

Other cats rose and stroked themselves against the bars, inviting some courtesy in return, or if too sick, if dying, looked at him from sunken eyes as they crouched in the backs of the cages. Phillip's laughter turned sharp-edged in his throat. But he reached in and touched each sick cat, and two responded with purrs and surprised looks of pleasure. "Yeah, it's still good," he said to the last one, as the bony gray head butted up into his palm. "It's still good."

He was careful to go back and wash his hands before touching the kittens.

They were frantic for the food, squalling, tumbling over one another, climbing the bars, and reaching out greedily, claws spread wide. Phillip sailed the dish over their heads into the back corner of the cage, and after a few seconds of frantic glancing about, everyone found it.

"Hungry, aren't they?" said Dr. Rossi, passing behind him. She was bringing Mrs. Farley to see her cat.

This was the gray cat that had purred at Phillip. He had feline leukemia, and after months of flickering up and down, his life-force had abruptly waned. He had been at the clinic for a week, living on injections. Mrs. Farley visited every day.

She brought the frail creature out now and stood holding him, with tears running down her face. The cat seemed uninterested, uncomfortable. He looked toward his empty, featureless cage, as if he wished to return to it.

"I recommend putting him down," said Dr. Rossi, bravely looking into the woman's face.

Mrs. Farley shook her head. "No, I couldn't do that," she said. "While there's life, there's hope."

There is no hope. Dr. Rossi didn't say it, but Phillip heard the words somehow hanging in the air.

Mrs. Farley gave her cat a last desperate, gentle hug.

She'd come for something that she hadn't gotten from him, and after he had crept back into the corner of his cage, she stood looking for a moment, in deep frustration. Then she started to leave.

"Better wash your hands first," suggested Dr. Rossi gently, and then, as Mrs. Farley stood drying: "A woman gave us these poor darlings to dispose of."

Mrs. Farley looked into the cage. Please, thought Phillip, moving away. Your cat will die, and so will all these kittens. You could save something! Mrs. Farley looked for a moment, saying nothing, and then went away.

CHAPTER FOUR

Phillip walked home.

The wind was slight, but damp, and raised goose bumps on his skin. He pushed his hands deep in his pockets and walked quickly, eyes down, seeing only the flash-flash-flash of his own sneakers in the dark. The thin material of his shirt clung and made him even colder.

The smell of roasting chicken and baked potato rolled out the door on a wave of heat. Phillip passed the kitchen area, where his mother was making gravy, and collapsed in his chair at the table.

"Phillip! Where's your jacket?"

"School."

"Well, for goodness' sakes, go wash up, and put on a sweater! Dinner's almost ready."

When he came back, the chicken was on the table, and his mother was slicing off a piece of breast, with the golden, crackly skin. She cut open a potato, and the steam burst forth. She scooped out the potato, buttered it, and put pats of butter into each half of the skin, then covered it with gravy. She added a spoonful of corn and some bread-and-butter pickles to the plate and carried it around the corner into the living room.

"Carl? Here's your dinner." There was the clack of

his tray being opened. "Wait, I'll get you a napkin." Not a word from his father. The only sound now coming from the living room was the television, turned very low.

"Now, eat that all up, or I'll feel bad! This is one of the chickens I raised this summer!"

A grunt from his father.

His mother came back around the corner. Her eyes were wide. She gazed at something not in the room, and she watched it as she served Phillip and herself and sat down.

"How was school?"

"Okay. Where's Thea?"

"She went out."

That was all the dinner conversation. His mother continued to stare ahead of her, and Phillip ate. He hadn't been this hungry in months.

"There's chocolate cake for dessert," said his mother when Phillip was slowly polishing off his third helping. She was a farm mother. Her whole life was based on feeding people.

Now Phillip was so full he ached; he was drunk with it. He rose from the table and went into the living room.

His father's plate was hardly touched.

Phillip perched on the rim of the couch, next to a dozen or so pillows needlepointed and embroidered with duck motifs, and looked, as his father did, at the television. The voices were barely audible. His father sat unblinking, never taking his eyes from the set even through commercials. The remote-control device rested on the arm of his chair. Phillip had never seen him change the channel.

"Carl. Please eat your dinner. You need to keep up your strength."

He looked at the TV tray in slight surprise and did begin to eat, but slowly, dutifully, as if it were hospital food. Phillip watched his father's hands. The fingers were swollen from years of work, and the palms were still hard, more like tanned leather than normal human skin. But they were pale now, with only a lingering yellowish cast from all the years of sun and frost, dirt, manure, and tractor grease.

He sneaked a look at his father's face. A brief look; he didn't like to see the thin, clear tube that came from behind his father's ear and entered his nostril: the oxygen tube. Only a few weeks ago that had not been necessary.

His father had had cancer, but the doctors operated and took that out. He also had something else, a mysterious lung condition from years of breathing the fumes from manure pits, breathing antibiotic dusts, herbicides, pesticides, cigarette smoke. He was losing ground faster than they'd expected.

"Carl?"

He had left a lot on his plate, but he looked up and said, "Good meal. Thanks." Tonight he sounded as if he needed to cough, good and hard, and clear his chest.

"Carl . . ." Phillip's mother wanted to talk, but there was nothing fresh to say. The two of them had spent all day in this house, with the television murmuring in the corner.

"One of . . . your chickens?" his father asked. Reaching out with his blunt thumb and forefinger, once as strong as a pair of steel pliers, he pinched off a piece of the golden, seasoned skin and tasted it.

"Yes," said Phillip's mother. "But you know, five of that batch of chicks had their legs all crippled up! I think I'll send away to the place we used back home, next year, and get some good old-fashioned Barred Rocks."

"Huh." His father reached toward the chicken again, changed his mind, and pushed the plate away.

"You like the Barred Rocks, don't you?"

No answer.

"Carl? They're pretty birds, don't you think?"

"Hmm? Yeah." He was looking at the television again.

"Well! What's on?" asked Phillip's mother brightly. Phillip got up from the couch and went outside.

The night air felt clean and cool, swelling his lungs. A simple pleasure, unavailable to his father and Mrs. Farley's cat. Phillip stared off down the row of street lights, wishing he were somewhere else.

It was always like this—worse now, since his sister, Carrie, had left for nursing school. His days were like sandwiches: a huge slice of dry, fluffy boredom on top; another slice of airless suffocation and silence on the bottom; and between, the clinic, a thin spread of life—blood and shit and pain and sometimes, the miraculous flood of health back into an ailing body.

It had been a summer job, mainly for relief, and he'd hung onto it because it was the only place, outside soccer class, where anything seemed to happen to him.

Not today, though. Definitely not today.

He crossed the breezeway and opened the garage door.

The garage was stuffed with the overflow of their former life. It had a discarded, musty smell, like the kitchen of the gray house.

In a corner Phillip found what he was looking for. Ax. Chain saw, splitting hammer, wedges. The chain saw was dirty with oil and sawdust, the ax and hammer handles polished by long wear—formidably useful, in this suburban neighborhood that had no use for them. There was also a log from the dying maple they'd cut at the end of summer.

He was all set, then, and he'd wait at the corner tomorrow for Kris's father. He'd assume he was going to be picked up. . . .

Thea, the black and white cat, slipped past his legs. Phillip grabbed her before she could disappear into the labyrinth of furniture.

"Time for you to go in." He dumped her through the kitchen door.

Flick! went her tail. She turned and stalked into the living room.

"Thea!" cried his mother. Thea's tail went straight up, and her back rose a little. Her gait changed from angry slouch to charmed, and charming, amble.

"Hey, puss!" A whisper from his father, *s*'s hissing. Thea leaped onto his lap, and his big hands, which had lain idle all day, stroked and stroked her. She lay back on his knee and beamed up into his eyes, purring.

"There, puss, there, puss," he whispered. "There, puss."

"We have three kittens at the clinic that somebody dumped," Phillip said. "I think we have to kill them tomorrow."

"Oh, dear," said his mother. No one—not his mother, not his father, certainly not Thea—said, "Bring them home."

Phillip went and took a warm shower. He left the light off and in the dark turned his face up to the shower head. The water beat on his cheeks and slid down them, and if he had been crying, he would not have felt the tears.

CHAPTER FIVE

I n the morning Phillip waited on the corner, his tools in a grain bag and the log at his feet. Wind sneaked through every seam of his clothing, and the world around him went light and dark and light again, as giant clouds sailed majestically before the rising sun. He and Carrie used to turn cartwheels while they waited for the bus at the end of the long farm driveway. Phillip hadn't felt like doing that in a long time.

Carrie was coming home for the weekend; that was the one thing his mother told him over breakfast, after she asked what he wanted in his sandwich.

The car came. Greg, beside his father, looked out on Phillip in lofty boredom. Kris was in the back, reading. She glanced up with a hard-eyed, don't-care look. Normally Phillip would have wilted and turned away. This morning he felt brave and strong and flashed her a cheeky grin. He watched her eyes widen and her face flush and saw her eyes falter down to her book. An unexpectedly sad feeling pierced Phillip's excitement.

I don't really know you, he thought. And you certainly don't know me.

Did anyone ever know anyone else? He avoided wondering about his parents and Carrie, but then there was no one left to consider. No one but Thea, and of course he didn't know her.

On the other hand, it was pleasant to think that he didn't know Greg and didn't need to. Count your blessings, Johnson!

☐ ☐ ☐

The log shed beetles and dark, crumbly bark on the orange carpet. The teacher, troubled and dubious, made Phillip spread newspaper underneath.

He split the log first with wedges, popping it open neatly. It had a nice straight grain. No one had ever seen the heart of this tree trunk before; no one had touched this fresh, bright wood. His father pointed that out once. People always said it about a gemstone newly pried out of the earth, but it was as true of a piece of wood, his father said.

He split the log in quarters with his ax, mainly for the pleasure of it, and split one of the quarters into kindling, mainly for the grade. Kindling he had plenty of.

"See you on the bus," he said later, passing Kris on the way out of class.

Her eyes were sharp on him. "History," she contradicted.

He didn't answer. Everything was tumbled into his grain bag now: jacket and tools, wood, books, and lunch.

The sun was shining through the big front doors. Meeting Mr. Pilewski, the attendance officer, in the hall, Phillip looked him straight in the eye, smiled, and went out unhindered.

He took what he wanted, put the bag in the trunk of

Kris's father's car, which had been left unlocked for him, and stood there with the lid up, looking around. A couple of people were walking across the parking lot. Phillip put his jacket on and looked busy in the trunk. When he turned again, they were gone, the glass in the big front doors just shivering shut behind them. It was completely quiet now. He was the only person left. He picked up his ax and hatchet and started up the bluff.

□   □   □

When he reached the gray house, Phillip stood on the road for several minutes, looking. The exquisite loneliness of the place brought an ache to his throat. Perhaps he should walk on. It was a house that perhaps should be chance-met by wanderers, not returned to by a person with an ax and his lunch, and matches in an old baby-food jar.

But that feeling left him. The brook began to sound busy, and his eye drifted to the dead tree limbs he'd seen earlier. Time for work.

After the first few strokes the feel of using an ax came back to him—how the weight of the head and the length of the handle, and gravity, do the work for you. How effortless it seems when you do it right, until suddenly you find yourself tired. How your thoughts go away, your feelings go away, and you stand in physical clarity, your body and the ax and the log. Mindless labor. He had been missing it.

He chopped and carried wood indoors until he was more tired than he'd been in months, and starving. Then he sat on a rock by the brook and ate his meat loaf sandwich. It tasted wonderful, washed down with cold brook water. He felt perfectly blank. Nothing to hide. Nothing to prove. His only needs were biological and already satisfied. He just saw things, didn't even name them to himself.

At last, though, a tiny worm of worry invaded the airy blankness. As soon as he perceived it, Phillip knew how good it was to be blank. Too late. He had to look at his watch, and yes, it was time to go.

□　□　□

People were getting on the buses when he came to the top of the bluff. Despite his good intentions, he was late.

He dropped down the steep hill without holding back. Slap! His sneakers hit pavement, and he was sprinting across the parking lot, dodging between cars. Shouts sounded in his ears: people noticing him as they went to their cars to drive home. The shouts were wordless; the wind in his ears blew the words away.

As he angled behind his own bus, he heard the door close, the engine start to make a let's-get-moving sound. One of Phillip's knees buckled, but he lurched forward and banged the door with the flat of his hand. The driver glanced his way, casually pushed the handle to let the door open. Not his disaster if some boy missed the bus. Not his business to ask why the boy was late. Panting, weak-kneed but serene, Phillip slowly mounted the steps, made his way down the aisle, and dropped into the seat beside Kris.

Her eyes raked his face. If you were feeling vulnerable, that look of hers could almost seem to scratch you. Today Phillip felt unscratchable, as if his face were made of hardened steel. He leaned back against the seat, feeling cheerful, while his pumping heart ran down a little and his breathing slowly relaxed.

"I've got a pear," Kris said finally, touching her crumpled lunch bag. "If you're hungry."

"Not really," Phillip said, and almost smiled at her alert look. He imagined a sharp yellow pencil making a note in her squared, rapid script: Not hungry Friday. "Want to split it?"

The mental pencil paused. She met his eyes, and then took the pear out of her bag and handed it to him.

NO EATING ON THE BUS, said a sign up over the driver's head. The sign also prohibited swearing, smoking, and being in the aisle when the bus was in motion.

The pear was ripe and very good.

□　□　□

It took the clinic to bring him down: seven greyhounds that had blown their last chance in the Thursday Night Trifecta; Mrs. Farley's cat, whose pale, depleted blood could no longer carry oxygen, wailing for breath after his fluid shot; Dr. Franklin swearing at the sound, while tears trickled into his beard, later drawing Mrs. Farley gently aside to try to persuade her, still later flinging out of the clinic in a rage. . . . Soon the gray house was so far away that it might as well not exist. As Phillip knelt and wrapped his arms around a doomed greyhound, waiting for Dr. Rossi to kill it, he was surprised at the soreness in his shoulders and for a few seconds could not think where it came from.

"I hate to do this to you, Phillip," said Dr. Rossi when all the dogs were dead, "but I can't bear to deal with Hugh again. Will you bring me the kittens?"

Phillip turned, openmouthed. But . . . he thought. But . . . I'm a high school kid. I'm . . . I'm not . . . make *him*!

Feeling as if he were walking underwater, he got a clean litter box and put the kittens in it. Phillip tried not to look at them, but the feel of their round, sturdy rib cages was imprinted on his hands. He put the litter box on the table before Dr. Rossi and stood there herding the kittens back inside it as she filled her syringe.

She turned now. Her large, compassionate eyes crossed his face, paused, came back again. "Phillip?"

He looked away, and his eyes had to fall on the kittens.

"I'm sorry, Phillip. I shouldn't . . . quite often I forget how young you are." She touched his shoulder gently. "Go on. I can manage by myself."

Phillip shook his head. She couldn't manage—hold a squirming kitten *and* find a vein—and her compassion was misplaced. He would go on living.

He picked up the first kitten. The other two immediately scrambled out of the box and prowled to the edge of the table, with amazed expressions. The one in his hands squirmed, furious at being restrained.

Dr. Rossi approached with her needle. How sad she looked, like a lady in an old painting. Phillip pressed the kitten flat on the table. It let out a little, complaining mew, and he thought how he would like to lay his head on Dr. Rossi's shoulder and cry. She would let him—and that's what Dr. Franklin wanted, too, but she wouldn't let Dr. Franklin. . . .

He let the kitten up.

"Phillip?" Dr. Rossi looked at him again. Her large eyes were almond-shaped, with heavy lids and artful makeup. He loved to have her look at him.

"I'll take them," he said, watching her eyes. They looked puzzled—maybe a little annoyed?

"Why?" she asked.

Why? thought Phillip. He looked at the kittens, cautiously reviewing their options at the rim of the precipice. Unthinkable, to sink a needle into them and stop all their motion and discovery. But it was always unthinkable, and it continued.

He looked back into Dr. Rossi's eyes, wishing to say something, to see himself mirrored there. But he had nothing to say that would be bold enough to show up, only the sensation of a round, sturdy body in his hands, a confused feeling in his heart, and a secret resource.

He began putting the kittens back into the litter box. "Can I leave them here until office hours tomorrow?"

Dr. Rossi was frowning. "I don't like this, Phillip. We've been here before, and you can't keep on doing it."

Again he had no answer. He could only look at her mutely, thinking how beautiful her eyes were and hoping she couldn't read his thoughts, spreading his hands wide to keep the kittens down in the pan. Trying not to think ahead.

She shook her head in frustration. "Oh! You're as bad as Hugh, in your way! Put them back in the cage!"

CHAPTER SIX

All the way home Phillip tried to make his brain consider what he'd done and what it meant for the future. His brain refused to consider at all. It glossed right over the strange car in the driveway and had forgotten completely that Carrie was coming home. But there she sat at the table, perking up the whole room with her blond head of curls and her animated face. Someone else sat there, too, back to the door—a guy.

"Oh, hi, Phlip!" Carrie said, checking with the other person as she spoke his silly nickname. "Wow! You really work late!"

"Hi," said Phillip. The kitchen was warm and smelled like leg of lamb with rosemary.

"Phillip, I want you to meet somebody," said Carrie, her eyes checking with the somebody again. "This is Derek Hansen. Derek, my little brother, Phillip. Derek is studying to be a nurse, too."

A nurse! thought Phillip, moving so Derek's face came into range. Oh, well, nothing wrong with that, said the liberal, modern, and tolerant section of his brain, correcting his first surprised thought. But tolerance and adjustment came to an abrupt end when he got a look at Derek.

It couldn't be easy for a guy to go into something like

nursing. He could do it because he really cared about people and had a need to help them on a personal, physical, day-to-day level. Or he could do it because he'd be certain of getting a lot of attention and getting girls. Looking at Derek's smug, smiling face, Phillip was sure he knew which.

Typical Carrie! For a beautiful girl she wasn't nearly skeptical enough about the male character.

Of course, she was head over heels in love. Phillip had seen it before, but never worse than this. She was explaining about his job at the clinic now, in a tone of voice that made him sound like an exceptionally clever five-year-old. Phillip squirmed inside.

"So, Care, how's school?" he interrupted.

"Oh, *great*! I really like it!"

Too many exclamation points. Carrie wasn't an exclamation point girl.

"Think you're gonna like spending the rest of your life with sick people?"

His mother dropped a spoon on the stove top. Derek swung his bored hazel eyes to look at Phillip, as if noticing him for the first time, and Carrie flushed angrily. In the sudden silence they could hear the murmur of the TV in the living room and the sound of his father's breathing.

"Sorry," said Phillip. "Bad question!"

"As you can see, Derek, my brother can be quite the little jerk!"

"Oh, no," said Derek. "I think it's a good question, actually."

The anger drained from Carrie's face. She gazed at

Derek respectfully, waiting for the pearls of wisdom to drop from his lips.

"It's something you have to ask yourself," Derek went on. His eyes traveled from Carrie to Phillip: Am I holding your attention? You slimeball! thought Phillip, opening his eyes wide and gazing raptly. "For me," said Derek, "it comes down to being of service. As long as I know I'm helping, I can hack it. But it's tough." His eyes took on a look of suffering, and Carrie flushed with sympathy.

"What if you can't help?" asked Phillip. "What if they're dying, and that's just it?"

"Well, that's where faith comes in," said Derek, smiling.

The wail of Mrs. Farley's cat sounded in Phillip's ears. He thought how pleasant it would be to punch Derek.

"Derek's very religious," said Carrie proudly.

"Oh, yeah? What religion?"

"You probably haven't heard of it."

"Moonie?" asked Phillip.

"No, I belong to the Reformed Church of the Brethren," said Derek. His eyes were impossibly limpid and mild, but far from selfless. Derek was enjoying the way he handled his girlfriend's hostile little brother. Phillip held his own sweet smile in place with a great effort. He knew he could never outsmarm Derek, and he waited for something that would let him break off honorably.

His mother had the same idea. "Phillip, have you washed up? Supper's almost ready."

"Don't forget behind your *ears*!" said Carrie.

"Yeah, Care, I'll wash my mouth out with soap, too!"

He went into the bathroom, almost whistling. Anyway, it was good to have Carrie home.

In honor of the guest, his father sat at the table. He ate little. Derek served him obsequiously, jumping to hand him the potatoes, the gravy, the relish. Carrie watched her father, biting her lip, or looked at Derek with tear-filled, grateful eyes. The smiles Derek gave her in return were warmly encouraging, modest, and noble.

But try though Derek might, by dropped hint or direct question, he couldn't draw the sick man into conversation. He smiled when it seemed to be expected. He nodded kindly; but he seemed to be listening to something else, and his eyes never once sharpened on Derek in the old way.

Eventually Derek gave up on conversation in favor of monologue, glancing at Carrie from time to time as you might glance at your own handsomeness in a mirror.

This was fun, Phillip realized. Hating Derek gave him something interesting to think about, and listening to Derek was stimulating. It stimulated him to disgust and contempt, anyway, and that was better than nothing. He was rather disappointed after supper, when Carrie and Derek went for a walk.

"Save the dishes, Mom," Carrie said. "We'll do them when we get back."

Phillip watched them go down the driveway. Derek put his arm around Carrie's waist, and she hugged him, as if in sheer relief at getting away from her awful family for a few minutes.

Phillip did the dishes himself, over his mother's protest. She really had nothing else to do, and it was no treat to gain an extra half hour for television. But Phillip was then able to greet Carrie and Derek with a dish towel in his hand and a saintly-looking smile on his face. He'd invented it, using his reflection in the window over the sink.

He was in his room later, making a lid for his bike basket, when Carrie came in. She closed the door, but Phillip could still hear Derek's voice, explaining to their mother why he wanted to be a nurse rather than a paramedic or a doctor. Not enough guts, not enough brains, thought Phillip—unfairly, since Carrie had plenty of both—but Derek called it "a dedication to humble service."

"Phlip, why are you being such a jerk about him?"

Did she really want to know, Phillip wondered, or was she just positioning for the attack? He took a chance.

"He's the kind of guy that's always got one eye on the mirror. You know what I mean?"

"No, I *don't* know what you mean!"

"Yeah, you do. Derek cares about Derek, period."

"He also happens to care quite a lot about me!"

"You're just another mirror to him, Care. He checks with you to make sure his personality's on straight."

"Well, who *doesn't* do that, smarty? Who *doesn't* use other people to check up on themselves? What about you and your little friend Kris?"

No, thought Phillip. He didn't want to see himself in Kris's eyes. He usually assumed he was invisible to her, and then she got mad.

But don't ask me about Dr. Rossi!

"See?" said Carrie. Because he was silent, she thought she was winning. *"Everybody* likes people who show them in a good light!"

"So what does this guy show you back, Care, that you can't get from your average bathroom mirror? Huh? What does he know about you that *we* don't?"

"He *happens* to—"

"Carrie! Phillip!" Their mother stood in the doorway, looking distressed. "We can *hear* you out there!"

Carrie flushed deeply and turned away. A moment later Phillip heard the bathroom door shut.

"Aren't you two a *little* old for this?" asked their mother helplessly.

Phillip bent over his bike basket, waiting for her to go away.

"Couldn't you be a little nicer, Phillip? She's going through a very hard time. . . ."

"Yeah, sure," said Phillip, thinking: Why am *I* always taking the heat for everybody else's hard time? I'm supposed to be Superboy or something? The kid who can take anything?

Maybe he was invisible. Maybe he had such a flat personality, such an ordinary face that people passed right over him without noticing. He felt like a person cracking apart, but all anybody else saw was a vague shape, taking up space. Presumably the shape looked reliable since people kept trying to rely on it.

He heard his door close and realized that his mother had been standing there for some minutes, watching him.

CHAPTER SEVEN

Phillip awoke late, to an empty house. "Gone shopping, etc.," the note on the table said.

That was fortunate, Phillip thought. Now he wouldn't have to make up an explanation for being gone all afternoon. He'd disappear before anyone came back to be explained to.

After breakfast he got two pot-pie tins and a quart freezer bag of Thea's food and went out the door. He had a whole morning to kill before it was time to pick up the kittens. Go to Kris's and get his homework, he decided.

As he was putting the cat food and dishes into his bike basket, he saw Thea crossing the front yard. Phillip spoke; she didn't come. Since they'd given her the freedom to roam, she had turned away from them somewhat—a grown-up now, with business of her own. He picked her up. She stared at him with eyes the color of lemon slices, wild and empty.

"Hey," he said, "remember me?" She squirmed out of his arms.

Slightly melancholy, Phillip got on his bike and rode to Kris's house.

The car, the trunk of which held all his homework, was not in the driveway. No one was home.

Kris would be at Aunt Mil's house, working and talking. Aunt Mil, at eighty-three, was her best friend.

Which is weird, thought Phillip, biking lazily along the quiet streets. Yet when he was with them, the friendship seemed perfectly natural. Kris was more at home with grown-ups than with kids. At school she seemed out of place, too high-powered for the company she had to keep. Of course, there were parts of her life he didn't see, like the debate team. Maybe with Handsome Dan Morgan, Heidi Holler, and Alice Knapp, she fitted right in—

Almost without planning it, he found himself in front of the little brown house.

He could hear voices out in back as he wheeled his bike inside the picket fence. He walked slowly toward the corner, never completely stopping and so not technically eavesdropping.

". . . the opposite of anthropomorphism," Kris was saying.

"Exactly!" Aunt Mil's voice. "You would never expect an animal to give you something it doesn't have—you know better. But I think that distinct line you draw makes you expect too much of people. We don't always have the strength it takes to speak of things, or the self-knowledge either."

Kris made a disgusted sound. "Makes you wonder why we ever invented language if we aren't going to use it!"

"Use your eyes instead, Kris. You know how to observe animals—"

"Diana, *no!*" Kris interrupted. "Sorry, I think she hears a cat in the front yard."

Phillip glanced over his shoulder and then realized *he* was the cat. He lengthened his stride and walked around the corner, hoping he looked casual.

All three were watching for him: the tall, lean greyhound and the tall old woman, her face drawn with cold and her beaky nose especially prominent, and Kris, who flushed slightly and raised her chin and looked directly at him with an intent, determined expression. All three, creatures of prey. He felt like a rabbit, innocently blundering into the open. . . .

"Hello, Phillip," said Aunt Mil quietly.

"Um . . . hi." They were still waiting. "Um . . . my homework? The car was gone—"

"It's on my desk," Kris said. "You can just go get it. I've got work here."

"I could help . . ." Phillip said. He often came on the weekend, often helped, but he was never sure if he should be taking the work from Kris, and right now he wasn't very sure of his welcome. The place was so attractive, though, with its neat garden beds, the cold frames, the berry bushes—so fruitful, so loved and utilized, unlike the featureless lawns of most nearby houses—that he had to try and stay.

Aunt Mil looked thoughtfully at him and then at the wheelbarrow. "Yes, you could help. You could fill this with leaf compost and dump it next to a rosebush—"

"And keep doing it till you drop!" said Kris with a sudden laugh, looking around the yard at the many unmulched bushes.

"And keep doing it as long as you wish to," said Aunt Mil, giving her a quelling look.

The composted leaves were black and crumbly, pleasant to handle. And the atmosphere in the little brown yard was pleasant, too: not much talk now, but an easy feeling and no stares from Kris. Phillip hoped it was going to last.

The sky was stony gray above them, and the day seemed to grow colder as they worked. Phillip's hands were red and his nose dripping before Aunt Mil decided it was enough.

□   □   □

In the living room, with a cat on his lap and his hands warming around a mug of cocoa, Phillip listened to the talk: dog training and Kris's father.

"I don't get it," Kris said. "All of a sudden he's really interested in Diana, but he won't admit it. He talks about this stuff at supper like it was an abstract concept, but it's always relating to something I did with her a few days before—and I don't know how he knows. Do you think he's spying on us?"

Aunt Mil shook her head. "He's quick enough to pick it up from day-to-day observation."

"But why is he interested?"

"Can't help it," said Aunt Mil. "He's interested in nature, and he's interested in you. You're the favorite child, you know."

Kris had just filled her mouth with a gingersnap, but she managed a profoundly incredulous sound.

"Oh, yes. You do things. Greg is all camouflage, and Amy is—who knows? But you and your father are very much alike."

"We are not!"

"You wouldn't see it, of course." Aunt Mil turned to Phillip. "And what have you been up to?"

Caught off guard, Phillip could only stare blankly back at her. What *had* he been doing? He glanced at Kris.

"Don't ask me," she said lightly.

"Um—" Phillip groped. "Ah, my sister's home for the weekend. With her new boyfriend."

"And you're here," said Aunt Mil.

"Yes," said Phillip, wondering if perhaps it was time to go. But it wasn't time to get the kittens yet, and besides, here were two people who would thoroughly appreciate Derek. He began to explain.

CHAPTER EIGHT

When Phillip arrived at the clinic in the early afternoon, a little girl and her mother were leaving. Behind them Dr. Franklin held the door, beaming, ushering them on their way. The mother led a dachshund and wore a dazed, slightly dubious expression. The little girl carried a kitten.

It was one of *his* kittens. He could tell from the new, shining look in the girl's eyes how she treasured the kitten against her chest. And he could tell by the guilt-stricken look on Dr. Franklin's face when he glanced up and saw Phillip.

"Nice kitten," he said to the girl. She didn't hear him—on cloud nine, in love. Little girls could be so intense. Dr. Franklin heard, though, and flushed a deep red on the few inches of face visible above his beard. Then he stared hard at Phillip and saw he was being teased.

"You shit, Johnson!" he murmured under his breath, waving a hearty good-bye to the unresponsive pair.

"You could get in big trouble like that," Phillip told him, going inside. "Giving away other people's animals!"

"So look me dead in the eye and tell me you really wanted three kittens!" They passed through the empty waiting room, where Sharon was on the phone. She caught Dr. Franklin's eye and scribbled a note on her pad. "Cassels canceled. Free 20 min!"

"Great, thanks," said Dr. Franklin, swooping past the desk. "You want combination shots for these guys, Phil?"

"Um—"

"I'll only charge you the cost of the serum," Dr. Franklin assured him. "You're on my free twenty minutes."

"Can they have a rabies shot?"

"Too young." Dr. Franklin scooped out the two remaining kittens. They burst into purr, like far-off motorcycle engines.

Phillip glanced into the cage of Mrs. Farley's cat. It was empty.

"Where—"

"Dead," said Dr. Franklin.

"Oh. Um . . . when?"

"This morning." Dr. Franklin plunked the kittens down on the polished table. "Hold these guys, will you, Phil? Don't just stand there with your hands hanging down!"

Phillip corralled the kittens and stood looking down at them. Their eyes were changing color. Earlier they had been grayish buff, like the inside of a blueberry. Now they were clearing and becoming yellow, losing that perpetually astonished look. Tigers; all the stripes they would ever have were crowded onto their fat little bodies. . . .

"Leukemia shots, too," he said, when Dr. Franklin came back.

"You want them tested?"

"No, just shots." What was he going to do if they had leukemia—kill them? They could have three years of good life. "Has Mrs. Farley come yet?"

"Mm-hmm." Shot for one kitten, shot for the other; Dr. Franklin's hands were steady, his face perfectly concealed behind the beard. He turned away now to get the leukemia shots.

"Are you going to be in trouble?" Phillip asked.

Dr. Franklin didn't pretend not to understand. He stopped moving, with his back to Phillip. After a minute he sighed, and his shoulders dropped. "No," he said.

"She didn't suspect." He turned around. "Let me test them, okay? Let's not spread this disease any further."

"They won't be with other cats—"

"You can't know that. No charge."

"It's not the money—"

"Oh—so you just don't want to know! Can you live like that, Phil?"

Hell, yes! thought Phillip, looking away. Everybody lives like that! Ignorance is bliss, remember? He could feel Dr. Franklin's gaze upon him. The guy never gave up.

"Oh, go ahead!" he said.

"Good!" Dr. Franklin turned back to his table for a syringe. "I wouldn't worry, by the way. The rest of the litter have all been negative. And anyway, it's not like you love them yet."

"True," said Phillip, letting one kitten go free for a moment and holding the other, so Dr. Franklin could draw blood.

But it wasn't true, really. He loved kittens immediately, without needing to become acquainted. To a kitten, everything was fresh, everything amazing. And everything was potentially fun—a toy, very likely, a wonderful game.

"I like them pretty well, actually."

Dr. Franklin looked up and made a face. "Do you know how many kittens there are in the world?" he asked. "All alike."

"So?"

"So—so I don't know. What's one kitten, more or less?"

"I don't know. Why did *you* take one home?"

"I cooked it and ate it for supper, Johnson! Don't be a wise-ass!"

Phillip collected the second kitten, which was exploring a nearby cabinet. He was reminded, suddenly, of his father finding a nest of kittens in the barn. Generation after cat generation this occurred, season after season. He remembered the smile on his father's hard, tanned outdoor face, the jaw glittering with stubble. It was as if he had just discovered something that proved once and for all the goodness of life.

"There," said Dr. Franklin. "We'll dock your pay next week for this. You got a carrier?"

"No, I'll take them in my bike basket."

Sharon poked her head through the door. "Hugh, Mike Andrews is here with his dog."

"Okay." Dr. Franklin scooped up a kitten and led the way through the waiting room. "Be right with you, Mike." He treasured the kitten against his chest, exactly as the little girl had, except that his expression was one of loving cynicism. Phillip had seen exactly that look in the eyes of a mother cat when her kittens were no longer new.

"They gonna be warm enough?" Dr. Franklin glanced at the goose bumps on his arm, then at the milky November sky. "Wait a minute, I'll give you an old shirt."

The flannel shirt he brought from his station wagon didn't look all that old. He helped Phillip tuck it around the kittens. One sat squarely in a pot-pie tin, and the other had started to tear into the plastic bag of cat food. Phillip took the bag away and tucked it into his pocket.

Dr. Franklin glanced curiously at these arrangements and then off at the sky. "Good luck, Phil," he said. "If you need anything . . . you know . . ."

"Thanks," said Phillip, and mounted his bike. He pushed off amid the loud, excited mewing of kittens calling for help.

□ □ □

They cried the whole long climb from the clinic to the high school driveway and beyond, along a road that became smaller and emptier and wilder and was completely unfamiliar to Phillip. He had never gone past the high school, even once.

It was a very different world from the one below. There were few houses, only thick woods on either side or weedy pastures. The farm was near the school, Phillip knew, but the road seemed to be carrying him miles out into the countryside. He was about to turn back when he came to a crossroad.

He stopped and looked all three ways. The roads seemed empty and devoid of meaning. He saw no sprinkling of manure, such as a spreader trails behind, and though a fresh, cold breeze was beginning to blow, it carried no cow or silage scent.

Almost at random he chose a road and pushed along it. It wound uphill and at last curved into a very small village—four houses and a little store with a gas pump out front. Phillip turned back.

Now he heard screeching tires and a loud, unmuffled engine, a long way off. It panicked him. Ever since he'd turned off the main thoroughfare, the roads had been empty. He pedaled madly for a hemlock up ahead and slipped behind its heavy boughs just as a sports car squealed around the corner. It ripped past him without pause.

He rested there awhile, listening to the jays and to the kittens, watching the vast, empty sky. Tiny white clouds made delicate patterns across the gray. After a while he heard another car and waited for it to pass before coming out.

At the junction again he tried another road, not very hopefully. How different this was from his aimless walk of last week, which had brought him to precisely the right spot in the world, as in a dream. . . . As in a dream.

He *had* dreamed that house once before. Perhaps he was going mad and had simply walked out of school into a dreamworld. Now awake, cycling down empty roads under a cold white sky, he was looking for something that did not exist, losing himself. His mind was going empty as the roads, cold as the sky. . . .

He felt the blood drain from his face. A bar of black started to rise from just below his vision, his head tilted helplessly—

Schplock!

As if at the flip of a switch, the light came back on inside his head. He looked around in confusion, braking slightly.

Schplock! Now the tire was streaking greenish brown before his eyes, and a familiar smell rose. He had entered a valley. A wooded bluff rose on his right, out across a dreary, stubbled cornfield, and ahead, peeking above a grassy knoll, was the top story of an old red barn. What he had just ridden through was cow manure.

Suddenly he was in the middle of the familiar scene. The barn lights were on now, the radio playing and the milking machines at work. Bony black and white backs of cows showed through the row of small square windows. The collie raced toward him with its silly, high-pitched woof.

"*Chipper!*" a woman yelled from the barn doorway. The dog, still expressing its doubts, circled back toward her. Phillip lifted a hand in greeting and thanks and swooped around the bend, along the rutted road that led out through the cornfield. Now that the dog was quiet, he could hear the kittens hissing.

"Sorry, guys," he said. "Not long now!"

The bike bumped slowly over the wet ruts and ridges. There was frost inside those ruts. He could feel it crunch and give, with a texture like chocolate-oatmeal no-bake cookies.

"I'm *hungry!*"

"*Mewp! Mewp!*"

And you're whacked, Johnson! That wasn't the kind of thing he'd say aloud, even to himself. But to be cycling cheerfully along now, over the ruts and puddles of this ugly farm road, when minutes ago he had nearly fainted from thinking he was crazy—yes, whacked. Not too extreme to say that.

□   □   □

At last he reached the house, knelt at the cold hearth, and opened the bike basket. The kittens looked up, eyes huge and silky whiskers curved forward. One cried. Phillip saw into its perfect little mouth: white, sharp teeth and rosy tongue. He lifted them out onto the floor.

They skulked around the bike basket, tails fluffed, ears flattened, met each other at the corner of the basket, and hissed.

Now they made wider circles, gradually growing taller and sleeker. Then a mouse rustled in the leaves beneath the kindling pile. Both kittens were there instantly, looking and listening so hard that their ears quivered, their whiskers quivered. Misfortune was forgotten. Phillip had to smile.

He took out the two dishes and filled one with cat food. The kittens' ears twitched toward the sound. They glanced partway, divided between the certainty of cat food and the mysterious lure of mouse. Then the smell reached them, mouse was forgotten, and they were crunching.

Phillip went to the stream and filled the other pie dish with water, got it back to the house without spilling more than half. The bike basket could be their bed. Phillip fluffed up Dr. Franklin's shirt and, when that still seemed meager, reluctantly added his own sweater to the nest.

Instantly he felt cold. Only a turtleneck for the long ride home . . . He almost took the sweater back but looked at the kittens, exploring in a corner with their pencil-point tails at half-mast, made a disgusted face, and didn't.

"See you tomorrow," he said. "Stay in here, okay?" He picked them up and felt the purrs vibrate through their round, sturdy bodies, kissed them, and put them in the box. Surprise! Oh, wonder! said their wide eyes, and they kneaded the wool for a few seconds. But then adventure called, and they jumped out again.

"Okay, but that's your bed!" Phillip told them. "Bye!" He closed the door tight behind him and remembered the back door, standing open. He said in a scolding voice, "You guys need names!"

CHAPTER NINE

He walked swiftly down the hill. Gravity alone moved his legs. He was loose-jointed and passive.

And invisible. He could see the black bulk of tree trunks and lighter spaces in between, and he could see mysterious shapes, like lurking bears, which turned out to be rocks or stumps. But it was mainly, suddenly, dark, and all he could see of himself was the white flash of sneakers, far below. Between his head and his feet stretched a long, dark, empty space.

Very empty, said his stomach, turning around and looking within itself for something to digest.

At the farm they were still milking. Phillip paused in a square of light from a window and flipped the tiny generator that powered his headlight into position against the back tire. When he pushed off, it cast a thin beam ahead of him, like a flashlight, wavering with the strength of his stroke.

Beyond the crossroad a few cars began to pass him, some roaring by, others creeping uncertainly, bewildered by the wobbling light. A man yelled, "Think anybody can *see* you, asshole?"

Ahead the sky glowed, unwholesome grayish orange, and soon he could see the swift car lights, white and red. Almost home.

□   □   □

They were all at the kitchen table, looking at him. Even his father was looking.

"Phillip, where have you *been*?" cried his mother.

Phillip glanced at the clock on the wall. Six-thirty.

"I . . . got lost," he said, to the front of eyes. Carrie's narrowed. Better than anybody else, she knew when he was lying.

"You're not even wearing a *sweater*! Do you want to catch your death of cold? You're old enough to know better, Phillip!" Angrily his mother got up from the table. "Get in the shower and then *put* a *sweater* on. Honestly!"

Phillip slid out of the room, away from the eyes. His mother's were only angry, but Carrie's were like weapons, and Derek's laughed in a nasty, teasing secret way.

His father's eyes, too, tired but a little curious. Least of all could he bear his father's eyes upon him.

He knew what would happen after supper and postponed it as long as possible. First, he helped wash the dishes. Then he settled down in the living room, face turned toward the murmuring TV, and listened to Derek talk about himself.

But his head was swimming with exhaustion. Carrie went out to the kitchen to get a snack for Derek, and Phillip slipped off to bed.

By the time she walked in he was under the covers. She closed the door behind her.

"You little creep, Phillip!"

"G'night, Care!"

"No, you listen to me!" She leaned over the bed. Phillip remembered what it was like when she was his big sister and could frighten him. "Why do you have to be such a little *jerk?* Don't you think Mom's got enough to deal with right now?"

Here we go again. Shelter Carrie. Shelter Mom. For God's sake, shelter Dr. Franklin, and Dr. Rossi! "It was *six-thirty,* Care!"

"It was *dark!*"

"So? There aren't any bears out there!"

"You know what I'm talking about, you little crudball!" She was getting more furious by the second, as none of her angry words killed him. In the old days she'd have jumped on him any second now, pinched him hard, or given him a knuckle punch. Now she wouldn't do that, but she'd do something, and as Phillip lay there, smiling his most irritating smile, he wished he knew what. Maybe he should just give up before she hurt him.

She said, "Dad's *dying*, you know! He isn't going to get better!"

Clever Carrie! He couldn't keep smiling in the face of that.

"Don't you think you owe it to them not to make trouble?" she asked. "Don't you think you could make the *sacrifice* of getting home in time for supper? You could spend the time with Dad; he won't be around forever!"

"Carrie, he might live for *years!*"

His protesting voice seemed suddenly too loud. Carrie stared at him, her eyes widening with shock. Phillip was shocked, too, but he didn't know why. Now he was afraid. The quarrel had gone too far, like a car swooping fast around a corner. He felt the nearness of the void. . . .

"Yes," Carrie whispered. "He might."

□   □   □

When she had gone, Phillip lay still under the blankets. The air vibrated around him. He could hear it, and he could see it, tiny particles dancing.

"Carrie, he might live for *years!*"

"Yes, he might."

"Carrie, he might live for *years!* . . . *years!*"

"Yes, he might."

"Carrie . . ."

CHAPTER TEN

Phillip awoke aching. His ribs felt compressed and meshed together. He opened his eyes. Thea, on his chest, gave a thin, rusty cry and started purring.

"Oh, God." He tried to move her, but she resisted, becoming instantly heavier. He groaned. Every breath was painful. *"Mee,"* said Thea, smugly.

Beyond his door he could hear the house stirring—his father's cough, the clash of dishes, voices. Carrie.

He rolled over, tumbling Thea off, and pushed his head deep into the pillow, pulled the blankets over his head. Within the dark cave last night's scene played through again.

"He might live for *years!*" And Carrie so shocked.

"The mark a kitten made, covering up its pee. I wrote it up for my brief but moving paragraph."

"Where did you see this?" Kris asked. She didn't look up at him, but the side of her face was suddenly still and alert. Ambush!

"On a road," he said. "On a dirt road."

"Oh." She continued to look at the sun symbol. "It's neat. Hopi, or something."

"I think it's on some state flag," Phillip said. He closed his notebook, took out a pencil, and carefully drew the little sun on the cover. He put a banner around it, rippling martially in the breeze.

"My coat of arms."

□   □   □

It was a perfect day for soccer. A perfect day for running laps, in a slow, efficient, pleasurable rhythm, feeling the blood begin to move and breathing in the crisp fall air.

He waited, relaxed, while the teams were chosen. Greg was a captain, of course, and Phillip was surprised when Greg's glittery dark eyes rested on him for a second, then moved on. The person he picked was not as good a player. Odd—Greg never did anything to jeopardize his chance of winning.

"Johnson!" The other captain picked him quickly, taking advantage of Greg's mistake. Phillip drifted over to that group and the yellow vests, remembering how Greg had looked up from the couch last night, remembering his own internal alarm.

The other fullback was weaker, but from the moment the whistle blew, all Greg's drives battered against Phillip's position. It was down that side that he chose to make his drives, as if there were no Phillip Johnson in the way.

But Phillip *was* in the way. He was not as good a player as Greg. He had a talent for obstruction and an instinct for where the ball would go next. Time after time they battled it out, eye to eye, shoulder to shoulder, and when Greg's eyes grew hot with anger and frustration, Phillip composed his own face into bland innocence. He knew it was infuriating.

Thus, when something changed in the last six minutes of the game, he wasn't really surprised. The three best players brought the ball down, passing it off between them. Stubbornly Phillip followed it, though the threat prickled along his body whenever he turned from Greg. Near the goal he went for the ball. It flew past him, diagonally to the other outside man, and the man in the middle, Greg, ran over him.

It was a hard hit, from behind. Phillip went down, hearing the smack of the ball against the goalie's shins; went down kicking, and hurt his toes on some part of Greg's body.

He rolled over and sat up. His elbow was bleeding, and his shoulder was going to ache; but Greg sat near him on the grass, surprised, holding his shin. So Phillip held his toes, though they didn't really hurt much, and assumed an expression of surprise himself.

"All right, guys?" The coach was coming over, and they stood up.

"Better get those brakes checked, Greggo!" said one of the hotshots, jogging past. He gave a friendly nod to Phillip. "Good game, Johnson!"

Phillip limped back to position. Good game, Johnson. He had slipped into this school almost without being noticed, which was exactly okay, but he was pleased, and he was pleased when the ball was put into play and the drive came down the other side of the field, brought by a player with only scoring on his mind—and the whistle blew.

Greg was still limping, so Phillip kept the little limp in his own walk. This was a civilized country school. Even being this provocative, he knew he wouldn't get knifed in the showers.

Later, with a carton of milk in his coat pocket, he walked openly past Mr. Pilewski, joining the flow of legitimate early leavers.

Good game, Johnson. . . . He felt great. A spring in his step and a chicken sandwich in his pocket; a destination; an enemy. You are defined when you have an enemy. Making one is taking a step in the world and can feel as good as making a friend.

He remembered Chuck ("No Relation") Johnson, more clearly than he remembered Rob or Billy Kennett, his best friends. Chuck missed him. In one of Rob's letters—to which he had not replied—he'd learned that Chuck still asked about him. "So how's that little jerk Phillip these days? Anybody stepped on his face yet?"

He hadn't written Rob simply because he had nothing to say. His old self had melted away like a snowflake on a hot truck hood. Now he thought of telling Rob about the soccer game. So many words, one after another . . . so different than if Rob had seen it. But maybe he'd do it anyway. "Tell Chuck that somebody has tried it. He says he'll try again when he gets the cast off!"

□   □   □

The kittens were in the bike basket, totally abandoned to sleep. When he spoke, they stretched and purred, slitted their eyes, and blinked at him warmly.

"Hey, guys! What if I was a fox?" He picked them up, still limp with sleep, cuddled them a minute, then gave them milk and food. The food dish was empty again, and he wondered if they were getting it all or having help from the local wildlife. They seemed fat, though.

He went outside and sat on the front step. The sky was brilliant blue today. Far up in the heavens the black locust branches traced scraggly lines, like trees in a Chinese drawing. Phillip saw a crow flap across the sky, and he saw it turn its head in flight to look at something to the east, without changing direction. He had never seen that before.

He took the sandwich out of his pocket and slowly began to eat it.

"Mew!" Suddenly one kitten was climbing his back, and the other was halfway up his chest, both going for the chicken sandwich. Hastily Phillip raised it above his head. The kitten on his back climbed onto his head, reaching up his arm. The other one looked around frantically, spotted the second half of sandwich on his lap, and rappelled down the front of his jacket toward it.

"Hey!" He snatched the second half aloft. "How'm I s'posed to *eat?"*

"Mew! Mew!" Desperate round kitten eyes coming toward his face, as the front kitten climbed his jacket again. He snatched a bite of sandwich. While he chewed, the kitten's whiskers tickled his lips, bobbing along as it searched for an opening.

Phillip took most of the chicken out of one half of the sandwich and gave it to them.

"Call you two Bonnie and Clyde!" he said. "Or Frank and Jessie!"

□　□　□

He got back to school a little early and sat on the curb, hidden by a car hood, and watched the buses come in. When the school doors opened and people began to pour out, he got up and joined them.

Kris was looking out over the heads. She seemed to know just where to watch for him today, stared hard for a moment, and then looked away. It was like the beam of a searchlight, turned on and suddenly off.

He edged into line beside her. "Hi."

"Hi." Her voice was light and perfectly neutral. Now what? Phillip wondered. All of a sudden it was no problem? That didn't make sense. Kris didn't let go of things like that.

"Sorry," she said. "I ate my apple today."

What is she up to? Phillip wondered. She was almost smiling, and she hadn't smiled at him in days, now.

He slumped in the seat, feeling the hunger in his middle that half a chicken sandwich had only teased. The hunger was as good as a meal, reminding him of barbecues he had eaten, huge platters of spaghetti and meatballs. He laced his hands across the hollow spot beneath his ribs, feeling good as a very hungry wolf might feel.

"Greg was still limping this afternoon," Kris said. "I heard you ran into him."

"And stubbed my toe," said Phillip.

"Hurt yourself?"

"Not much. It was worth it."

He heard a very faint snort of laughter. Her face was turned so he couldn't quite see her expression.

He unlaced his fingers, with difficulty because the knuckles were swollen with cold and wanted to stick against one another, reached over, and took one of her hands out of her lap. It was astonishingly warm. He curled his fingers into the palm.

They'd never held hands before. At their most intimate they knocked shoulders, walking, or she leaned over him as they read something together. This had better not become a habit, Phillip thought. The hunger blazing through him made everything more keen, and just holding her passive hand had his heart pounding.

"Phillip . . . are you okay?"

He burst out laughing, loud enough to make the bus driver glance up into his mirror. "Yeah," he said. "Do you have a stick of gum, even?"

"No. No, I mean, in general?"

"Yeah. Yeah. I'm okay." On the soccer field, at the house beside the stream, sometimes even on the bus, he was okay.

□ □ □

At the clinic he was okay, too. Mrs. Farley's cat was gone, and all the kittens, except maybe his own two, had good homes. A note from Dr. Franklin said, "Leukemia tests negative." There were no greyhounds to kill and hardly any cages to clean. Dr. Rossi was in a sparkling mood, joking and laughing with everyone. It was one of those times when being a vet seemed like the most fun in the world. Phillip thought uneasily, at moments like this, about his grade point average.

CHAPTER TWELVE

Tuesday Kris wasn't in school, and Phillip was glad. He'd awakened with that sinking, hollow feeling of having made a big mistake quite recently, and it wasn't skipping school, it wasn't kicking Greg, and he couldn't remember any serious omission at the clinic. That left Kris, and his stomach lurched distinctly at the thought of her. Whoa! Go slow, Johnson!

But the debate team had a statewide meet today. They had left very early in the morning, and since there was no one to watch him at all, Mr. Pilewski's supervision beginning in the front hall, Phillip walked around the bus straight across the parking lot and vanished for the day.

It was so easy. Having no friends simplified life enormously.

He spent a pleasant, leisurely, even slightly boring day alone: cut some wood, played with the kittens, took a nap in the sunshine. Then he walked out to the road and hitchhiked to work. It felt dangerous to do it that way, not going back to school at all. It felt like one step too far. Phillip was in a mood to like that feeling.

A lady in a new Volvo picked him up. She had short, elaborately cut hair that looked stiff to the touch, expensive clothes, and bloodred fingernails. But she was nice, asked about his job, and then wondered, "Shouldn't you be in school?"

"I don't have classes in the afternoon," said Phillip. He felt high and loose, like a kite with a broken string. "I'm a teen entrepreneur," he said. "I'm saving money to invest in my own carpet-cleaning business."

"You're a teen bullshitter," said the woman, taking a pack of cigarettes from her trench coat pocket. She shook one out and lit up without ever looking from the road. "Want one?"

"No." He watched her puff. "My father's dying from that."

"Emphysema?"

"Kind of."

"I'm sorry to hear that."

They were silent for a few moments. Then she said, "You're a good kid, you know? Most kids would have started the why-don't-you-quit bit."

"I figured I made the point," Phillip said.

She gave a bark of laughter, coughed, and threw the cigarette out the window. Phillip felt an inner glow, a smugness that he was afraid spread all over his face. "Wise-ass!" the woman said.

□　□　□

He arrived at the clinic exactly on time, to find things in an uproar. There had been greyhounds. Sharon had had to help with them, and just before office hours she walked into Dr. Rossi's office with red eyes and blotched makeup and gave notice. "I just can't take it anymore."

"Well, what about *me*?" cried Dr. Rossi.

"It's your job!"

"It's your job, too!"

"Not if I quit," said Sharon, and marched back out to the desk.

There was no time for more talk. The first patient had arrived, a huge cat, brought in to have his claws clipped. Phillip was holding him when the cat suddenly jerked out of his grip and slashed a bleeding line across Dr. Rossi's arm.

"Please *hold* him, Phillip," was all she said.

"Oh, don't hurt him!" cried the owner as Phillip almost lay on the enormous, cursing cat.

"You could do this yourself, you know," Dr. Rossi

suggested, pausing to wipe a trickle of blood from her arm with a bit of gauze.

"Oh, *no*! He'd never forgive me. He's very sensitive, aren't you, Boss?"

Boss, though mostly squashed, managed to project a hind foot from somewhere and rake it across Phillip's stomach. A ripping sound accompanied, not all cloth. Phillip flinched, Boss writhed, all claws at full extension, and Phillip fell on him again. Dr. R., I hope you see what I'm suffering for your sake! When he straightened up afterward, there was a six-inch rip in his shirt and a long scratch across his stomach. Dr. Rossi was sympathetic, but not to the point of dressing the wound with her own hands. She gave him a bottle of disinfectant and headed him toward the bathroom.

Soon after that Dr. Franklin blew in, in a high state of irritation with every single one of his fellow beings. The news that Sharon was quitting sent him promptly to her desk, where he tried to conduct a whispered argument in front of everyone in the waiting room. Sharon burst into tears. Dr. Franklin retired to the storeroom to curse. Later he darted across the road to the supermarket, and at five o'clock, when the last customer had been shunted out the door, he popped out of the office to present Sharon with a bouquet of flowers, still wrapped in the original cellophane. She burst into tears again, and she and Dr. Rossi berated him on his attitude toward women. This ended with Dr. Franklin's loudly stated intention to go the bar in the motel next door and drink himself senseless. Sharon instantly said she would join him, unless he thought that women shouldn't be seen in bars. They swept out the door, and Dr. Rossi donned her stylish coat with the wide, wide shoulders and looked severely at Phillip.

"You stayed late eavesdropping," she said. "I'll drive you home."

As Phillip put on his jacket, he smelled again the Volvo lady's cigarette smoke. But in Dr. Rossi's little red car there was only the spicy scent of her perfume. Daringly, Phillip directed her to his house by the longest possible route. It was the most he could do. He could have ridden beside her, not speaking, for miles.

□   □   □

He walked into the kitchen and closed the door, and it was like a lid coming down. It shocked him how hot the house was, the smells of cooking all closed in—*good* smells, but too much—and how his mother prepared a plate and trotted it around the corner to his father, the tray clacked, murmur of TV. She scolded him, he ate a little. . . . From the moment he walked in, Phillip's free, expanded feeling began to narrow, and pressure built in him. How could it all be so *unchanged*?

"What did you do today?" he asked his mother.

"Oh, dubbed around as usual."

A few minutes later she asked, "How was school?"

"Huh? Oh. Fine. Where's Thea?"

It was then that he began to think of Kris again. She wouldn't be back till late. She was probably on the bus now, probably sitting with Handsome Dan Morgan. . . .

The TV was turned up so all could participate in the family activity. Phillip sat on the couch next to the duck pillows and hated Dan Morgan. He hated Kris, too, and Alice Knapp, and all the debate team—bused so far away, just to *talk* all day. Talk about anything—be assigned an opinion and defend it.

He'd be lousy at that. He defended himself with silence.

So he'd lose. At least he wouldn't be here. He wouldn't have his day of freedom, the wildness at the clinic, Dr. Rossi's perfume, all smothered to death inside him.

"Going for a walk," he said, and went to Kris's house, which looked like every other house on the street, gazed at her dark, blank window, and tried to breathe freely. But something pinched in the middle of his chest and stopped the breath. Clouds muffled the moon, and a raw breeze sprang up. Phillip went home again.

CHAPTER THIRTEEN

When he got on the bus the next morning, someone else was sitting with Kris.

Phillip hesitated in the aisle. There was not a single empty seat.

"Oh, here," said Kris offhandedly, patting the seat in front of her. The person sitting there was Dan Morgan; he was turned around, talking with Kris and Alice Knapp.

Phillip sat down beside him and tried to understand the conversation. The rules of debating were unfamiliar. At last he had to ask, "Did you win?"

Dan Morgan turned his head, faintly incredulous. "Of *course*, we won!"

In homeroom Heidi Holler took Dan Morgan's place, and the debate postmortem continued. Phillip took refuge in a book. Out the corner of his eye he watched Kris, and to his great shock he found himself thinking how beautiful she was.

No way! he thought. He'd first been attracted to her by moonlight, and in the light of day she had become a friend. He didn't think about what she looked like anymore, except to register alarm. She was too tall, too straight, like a young Viking. Not beautiful.

Yet he couldn't stop looking. She was lit up today, keen and excited. Even in the company of debaters, hers was the voice that cut through nonsense, that capped a sequence and got a laugh. She was brilliant, and proud, and yes, damn it, beautiful.

It would be nice if she spoke to him once in awhile.

He tried to work himself up to a state of indignation—tossed aside like a dirty sock!—but unfortunately it seemed only too natural. The debate team was a unit now, with things to talk about and victory to share. Phillip was what he'd always been, an outsider.

□ □ □

After gym he walked toward the front door as usual, passing Mr. Pilewski. A moment later he heard his name spoken: "Phillip. Do you have a reason for leaving school early?"

Phillip had actually forgotten that anyone had the right to stop him. He paused, eyes on the girl walking out ahead of him. A senior with no afternoon classes, she was assistant manager of a pizza joint. Her picture had been in the paper, in an article about high schoolers in the workplace. How can you fault these nice, straight kids for going out and making money? the paper had wondered. But when do they find time to study?

"Work," he said, slowly turning to face Mr. Pilewski. The man was a former football star, able to lift a fighting kid in each hand if necessary.

"Where do you work?"

"The veterinary clinic. Opposite the mall—"

"Oh, Madeline Rossi! She's great, isn't she?"

"Yeah."

"Look, get a note from her, will you, that you're working there afternoons? Just to put everything in shape?"

"Sure," said Phillip, putting an innocent puzzlement into his voice. He saw how that made Mr. Pilewski momentarily doubt himself, waved, and walked out the door and openly up the road.

Going by the road meant going the long way—long enough for triumph to evaporate. Phillip began to feel cheap. He never used to lie much. He remembered once wanting to, when a youthful experiment with a tractor had disastrous consequences. He remembered his father's direct look and heavy cuff and a lecture that made him realize exactly what a jerk he'd been. And then it was over.

Fixing the tractor had been fun actually. They'd worked late into the night, his mother bringing out coffee and sandwiches at ten, barn cats twining around, forgiveness and talk starting to come from his father as they grew more certain of making the repair. He remembered walking back to the house with his father, the stink of pig manure on the warm night air, and cutting it, a sharp curl of cigarette smoke, his father's hand on his shoulder.

Since he wasn't biking, he left the road early and skirted the edge of the cornfield. The mountain rose on his right, a dark bulk in the corner of his eye. To his left, the farm buildings receded into small bright paint spots across the expanse of brown earth and blond stubble. It took a long time to go around the field, and Phillip felt worse with every step.

Who would have dreamed, when his father stepped into the dark outside the barn that night and lit a cigarette, half his face reddened by the match flame, that the little curl of smoke above his head would change everything so soon?

Not just the cigarette. The hog smell, too, had done it. The gases from the manure pit below the hogs . . . It was against nature for animals to live that way, and it worked against nature, as if taking revenge.

Phillip toiled up the road to the gray house, clumped heavily down to the door, and pushed it open. No kittens. Dishes empty. He put down food, got water from the brook, and sat on the front step.

After a moment he heard cat food being crunched.

Wind picked up the locust leaves and whirled them around. Phillip's stomach whirled, too. He bent over, trying to squeeze it into stillness. He heard the wind and the cold, rushing sound of the brook, and they pained him like the memory of something lost.

Prrt! A kitten climbed the hunched back of his jacket. It stopped around his shoulder blades, and he felt by the small rocking motions that it washed its face and paws.

Rock, rock. The little thing weighed at most two pounds, yet Phillip felt how it moved his whole body. There was a secondary motion, smaller, quicker, and more regular, that after awhile he came to realize was his own heartbeat. Rock-rock-rock, his butt cold as ice on the cold stone step . . .

Suddenly he straightened, so quickly that the kitten had to scramble and grab hold. "Hey, where's the other one?"

He looked in the woodpile, rattled the food in the pie dish, called. The only response he got was that the kitten on his shoulder jumped down and began another meal.

Phillip crossed the rotten kitchen floor and looked out the open door toward the brook. The slope was bare and brown. Nothing moved, and when he called, his voice seemed to travel out infinitely, unheard, into the empty woods.

No point in searching. If it was dead, it was dead, and probably eaten, too. If it was just sleeping somewhere, it would emerge and greet him casually and make him feel like an idiot. If it didn't want to be found, he couldn't possibly find it.

While he made these calculations, he walked down the slope to the brook and stood there, looking into the woods as far as he could. He called again, hating the flat, hopeless sound of his own voice.

The first kitten bounced down the slope after him. When he saw how little it was, how it had to struggle through tangles of dry grass and leap scrambling onto small rocks, Phillip's heart sank. He had made a terrible mistake. This was no place for kittens. It would be hard enough for a grown cat to survive. He scooped the kitten up, laid his cheek on its soft fur for a second, and then let it settle on his shoulder, while he crossed the brook in long, hurried strides, shouting, "Hey! Kitten? Hey!" Every small stump or heap of leaves frightened and then disappointed him when he got close enough to see it was not a huddled body. "Hey! Cat!"

Finally he gave up. His toes were freezing inside his sneakers, and he couldn't tell if the vibrations of the kitten on his shoulder were purrs or shivers. He turned back, looking for the first glimpse of the doorstep. If it were Thea, that was where she would be.

The step was empty.

"Oh, *Jeesus*, what a day!" He felt tears sting the backs of his eyes. After all the fuss, all the work, the leukemia shots and the lying, the damned kitten had to get killed! He might as well take this one back. The needle was an easier death, probably, than being ripped apart and eaten. He pushed open the front door.

Instantly he heard it—thump-thump—the unmistakable small sound of a kitten jumping down from somewhere. As Phillip watched in angry, convulsive relief, the kitten came around the corner of the room, tail high. "Brrt!" it said, and headed straight for the food dish.

"Oh, for Christ's *sake*!" Phillip dropped the one kitten and scooped up the other, so suddenly that it squeaked. He turned it to face him, holding tight as it struggled. "You little *stinker*!"

Mew! The kitten was slightly alarmed and wanted lunch.

Helplessly Phillip glared at it. He wanted to bawl it out, punish it—*damn*! He held it, squirming, to his chest. He felt as if a hole had been scooped out there, empty and aching.

"*Eee!*"

"Oh, all *right*!" He put the kitten on the floor and watched the two of them eat. The damned kitten was *found*! Why did he still feel like this?

"It's not as if you love them yet." Dr. Franklin's

voice, in memory. "Do you know how many kittens there are in the world? All alike."

Could he lock them in? One look at the hanging back door, the holes in the floorboards, made clear the futility of that idea. It would be like trying to hold a handful of water, trying to hold life itself, keep everything still at one specific moment of his own choosing. Life leaked through the cracks—a car accident, a lung disease, a war, or just the steady march of time. . . . He sat down on the hearth, pressing his arms against his cramped stomach. "Shit! Shit, shit, shit!"

CHAPTER FOURTEEN

The next morning Kris was in the normal seat, and a place was saved for him. Dan sat with Alice Knapp some distance away. Phillip sat down. Kris found a piece of paper in her notebook and gave it to him. It was yesterday's history assignment. He sat staring at it.

"I wasn't on the bus last night," she said. "Were you?"

"Yes."

"I would have called, but there isn't that much. I didn't think it was worth you coming over."

"Oh." Not worth walking two blocks? Not worth escaping for a few minutes from his house, where he spent the entire evening silent in his room, hearing only the television and his mother's voice?

And anyway, what was going on here? Kris was reducing it to a system, and Phillip knew instinctively that it could not be a system. Any wrongdoing he'd ever gotten away with had been sporadic, occasional.

□　　□　　□

He'd decided to vary his pattern today, attend history as well as English, and eat lunch with Kris. But she had made an appointment with a teacher. As he was heading to the cafeteria alone, someone said, "Hi, Phillip." He turned to see a man catching up with him, a familiar face, but only that.

"How's it going?" asked the man.

"Fine," said Phillip, warily.

"How do you like our school now that you've been here a few weeks?"

"It's okay."

The man gave a shallow chuckle. "Only okay—I wish we rated better than that! Look, I like to meet with transfer students, just to get acquainted. How about we make an appointment for sometime tomorrow. Say, one-thirty?"

"I have—"

"You have study hall then. I checked." The man

smiled, narrowing his eyes in a friendly, jokey way that embarrassed Phillip into smiling back. "So—see ya then." He accelerated down the hall ahead of Phillip, and somebody said, "Hi, Mr. Peabody!" Mr. Peabody, the guidance counselor.

Phillip stood through the slow line to buy a milk and sat down at the last empty table, but his stomach was too twisted for eating. Yesterday Pilewski, today Peabody. Were they closing in on him?

"Mind if we sit here?" Four math team computer geniuses dropped into the chairs around him and continued their conversation. Phillip felt sick. He looked out the sliding door beside him.

The sky was gray, and the sun gleamed palely through the clouds, like a pearl. A wind rattled the stiff brown oak leaves.

"Excuse me," he said, standing up. None of the computer geeks appeared to notice. He went to the coatrack for his jacket and slipped out the door near the teachers' smoking area, currently uninhabited. He was blowing off French again, but he couldn't imagine sitting through it. Besides, he was fucked already. F for fucked.

He crossed the wide lawn and slipped into the trees, still in plain sight. A path was worn there, and Phillip started jogging. With luck, he'd pass for some ski team fanatic, getting a head start on conditioning. . . . In fact, two ski team fanatics went by him, running easily, their breaths making rhythmic white puffs on the cold air. "Hi," each said, in passing, and Phillip said, "Hi."

The trail they followed led straight up the ridge. The two runners scaled it easily, with no visible break in their rhythm. Far to the rear Phillip scrambled up, followed. He stayed near enough to see when they reached the dirt road and turned downhill, like good boys, taking the trail back to school. Phillip paused at the road, fighting the cold air as it seared his lungs. Then he turned uphill.

Still his breath hurt him, but he walked rapidly. Did his father's breath hurt? He didn't know—only that it didn't enrich the blood with oxygen as it should. How would that feel? Like breathing under a blanket, breathing inside a plastic bag . . . He passed the overlook to the farm and started uphill, his eyes down on the leaves.

Suddenly there were two rhythmic trampings in the woods: his own feet and someone else's. A fierce jolt of adrenaline rocked his body.

Straight ahead a short, wide man dressed like a soldier, in camouflage and high-laced boots, walked down the road toward him. The man carried a bow, and over his shoulder bristled the feathered ends of arrows. Larger and larger he loomed, as he and Phillip kept walking. Phillip's eyes were riveted on the black boots, the flashing brass grommets. Closer, closer—he glanced up at the face. Thick glasses, bristling red beard. A second later it registered on his mind that his eyes had just passed over a knife. The knife was short and wide like the man, strong and sharp and short.

"Hi," said the man, passing.

"Hi," said Phillip, a little late. They both kept walking, but in a moment, when Phillip paused and looked back, he caught the man turning away.

Quickly he walked on. He saw the wet leaves the man had scuffed up and realized how completely alone he'd always been up here.

He remembered now what he'd been seeing in school for weeks, without giving it a thought: the orange knit caps and orange vinyl vests of deer-hunting season. Bow season came first, and then regular season.

When? This weekend, he thought. The lonely woods would stir with men and boys and gunshots. The abandoned roads and the deer paths would be walked again, for two weeks, and it would not be safe to be out. He'd have to get himself an orange hat . . . but in case of accident, in case of a shooting by a careless, panicked boy who would run and never tell such a tale on himself, who would ever know where to find him? Another hunter might come upon him later, or perhaps not. Just last month a skeleton had been found in the woods, the remains of a man twenty years gone. He hurried to the gray house. Both kittens greeted him on the doorstep, mewing loudly for their dinner. Orange hats for them, too?

He hitchhiked to the clinic, where Dr. Rossi was tearing up Sharon's resignation, where Dr. Franklin and Sharon were organizing a greyhound adoption service, where things were for the most part remarkably easier than anyplace else in his life. People told him what to do, and nobody gave him time to think.

□   □   □

At home the sameness of the evening routine, the murmuring television, the hot, stuffy air, swallowed him up. It felt impossible to speak, and anyway, he had nothing to say. Neither did anyone else.

Thea came in late, when Phillip had given up hoping that Kris would call him about the French assignment and was consoling himself with a snack of cold pot roast. Thea rubbed against him briefly and then sat up, hooking her claws firmly into his jeans as she sniffed—reading him like a newspaper. Thoughtful, wide-eyed, she sank back to the floor and brooded. She was the only one around who had a clue about the kittens.

What else did she know about? Phillip wondered. Did Dr. Rossi's perfume linger? Did he smell less like school or Kris than usual?

Thea sank down, ears back, eyes glaring thoughtfully. Did a picture come into her mind of the kindling he had gathered and the wood he had chopped, of his frantic search through the woods yesterday? Did she have any notion, as she sat there brooding like a gypsy fortune-teller, of the complicated trap he'd set for himself, and when it might be sprung? Could she smell Peabody and Pilewski?

He scooped her up and cuddled her for a moment, against her will. She smelled of fresh air. Her fur trapped it and brought it indoors. . . .

She squirmed. "Oh, all right!" Phillip put her down. Immediately she rubbed against his leg. No hard feelings.

He shared the pot roast with her, allowing her to

crouch on the table beside his plate. They were civilized together. When Thea finished a piece, she would stretch out her paw and stop his hand, halfway to his mouth with the sandwich. He'd pull off another shred of meat and lay it before her, and she would sniff daintily and begin, with a short, eager purr. Thank you. "You're welcome, Thea." He kept his voice to a murmur, no louder than the television.

CHAPTER FIFTEEN

That night he awoke in the dark, eyes popping open, mind instantly alert, sat up, and turned on the bedside lamp.

Three-thirty in the morning.

Now what? Waking in the middle of the night was a sign of depression, but he didn't feel depressed now. He felt pissed off, and restless, and trapped.

Get up! That's what people say they're going to do when they can't sleep, but they never do.

As quickly, as precisely as if it were morning, he got out of bed and put on a shirt and jeans.

Real clothes made his waking state more real. He felt like going outside now, and he wondered how quickly he could bike to the gray house. There and back in three hours? He put on socks and padded down the hall to the kitchen.

"Phillip? Where are you going?"

Phillip's heart almost jumped through the top of his head. He turned to look through the living-room doorway. Wrapped in her bathrobe, his mother sat there at the far end of the sofa. She had the small light on and her needlework in her lap.

"How can you *see?*" Phillip asked irritably. He flipped on the rest of the lights.

"Where were you going?"

"Fresh air. Can't sleep. How long have *you* been up?"

"Oh, a while." She looked down at her work and carefully set another stitch in another damned duck.

"Why don't you get some *real* ducks?"

"I don't think the neighbors would appreciate—"

"Screw the neighbors!"

"*Phillip!*"

Phillip made a growl that was meant to sound slightly apologetic and went to the refrigerator. *Now* he felt tired. Gray spots danced before his eyes.

"Want some hot milk?" he asked. "Make you sleep?"

"No."

"Me neither." He closed the refrigerator door and passed the living-room doorway again. "Guess I'll try to sleep some more." His mother took another stitch. He had the impression that it was the first she'd taken since he passed out of sight into the kitchen. "Why don't you go back to bed, too?"

"I don't want to," she said. "I can always nap during the day."

True, thought Phillip, going into his own room. And no wonder she couldn't sleep! What did she do all day, but sit and stitch, and clean the clean little house? It was nothing for a person like her. He remembered her canning tomatoes, plucking chickens, making enormous suppers for the crew at corn-chopping time, staying up late working on accounts. She should go to nursing school, like Carrie, or marry another farmer. . . .

In the morning he wondered if it had been the change of weather that awakened him. The sky was clear, the air warmer, and a fresh breeze blew.

On the bus, Dan Morgan and Alice Knapp were sitting together again, talking softly, and he had the greyhound adoption plan to tell Kris about.

It was like setting flame to dry grass. Within minutes she was sketching battle plans. The greyhounds would need temporary foster homes until permanent places were found for them. Kris had every intention of providing one of these homes.

"It's an ideal situation. Diana can help socialize them, and there are no other pets for them to bother. But that means I can't—" She stopped.

"Can't what?" asked Phillip.

"Can't get a cat," she answered, after a moment.

"Were you planning to?"

"Oh, you never know!"

□   □   □

He had mostly forgotten his appointment with Mr. Peabody, but there was a note in homeroom to remind him.

He worried a little through English class, but today was the last day of soccer—last day, and a deep blue sky above, golden air that felt more like early October stirring up the leaves. While he stood waiting to be chosen and while he put on his vest, Phillip managed to keep thinking about Mr. Peabody but after that it was perfect.

Again he was opposing Greg, and that was good because Greg forced him to be brilliant. Today it was nothing personal. Greg couldn't be sure of winning and would rather stay cool. He butted up against Phillip's position occasionally, as if testing it for softness, but all his goals were made on the other side of the field, and after the game, passing, he said, "You should go out for soccer next year, Johnson." Phillip startled himself by seriously considering it, as he stood beside the bench zipping his sweatshirt.

"Nice game today, Johnson," said the coach, also passing. "Hey, Zebrisky, *cut that out*! Just because we all know you're an idiot, you don't have to act like one! Get me?"

Slowly Phillip followed the slowest person. He lagged until the gym doors shut behind everyone else. The coach's eye was on the usual troublemakers, and he did not check behind him for stragglers. Phillip pulled up the hood of his sweatshirt, put one hand on the bag of cat food in his pocket to keep it from bouncing, and jogged away.

He was more fit than ever in his life, like the boys in survival novels, hardened by their experiences. He admired himself as he climbed the bluff without a pause; maybe not as fast as those ski team runners, but just as steady.

Reaching the dirt road, he did have to stop and catch his breath. Then he walked on, striding rapidly. That was the day, breathing him along so lightly. It was his bare legs, the light breeze, the blue sky. He tried to worry, and indeed, deep in his heart was a worm of unease. But the day wouldn't let him stop.

"I have an appointment with doom," he said aloud, and skipped and kicked a stone.

He stopped at the farm overlook. Out across the broad flat expanse, the mud in the fields glistened, and in the barnyard the cattle, stimulated by the mild breeze, bucked clumsily and engaged in ponderous mock battle. The collie barked up at the cat, which washed its whiskers nonchalantly on top of a fence post. With the thaw the smell of manure rose very strongly.

On the road, just as the roof of the gray house came into sight, something stopped Phillip. He almost knew what it was; at least, he knew to turn back a few steps and look at the ground.

The sun symbol, drawn in the soft sand at the side of the road. Phillip stared at it, feeling again the strange thrill. It was like a sign from beyond the veil of the ordinary—order and beauty reaching through the mixed-up particulars of existence to tap him on the shoulder.

It's cat pee!

He felt the crazy grin on his face, the grin from the old days, when for a couple of people, for a little while, he'd been a ringleader and a total loon. He walked on to the house, remembering those times, then fed his kittens.

"This isn't the craziest thing I've ever done, you know," he told them. They were busy eating.

"Well, I can't stay and play with you guys," he said. "Got a date with doom!" He pulled the door shut, feeling a little guilty. They weren't getting much attention at this rate. What had he saved them for, anyway, if he didn't have time?

From, Johnson. Saved them *from*.

□   □   □

His timing was good. He got into the locker room at ten to one, the end of lunch period. He felt wide open, as if the wind of his running had swept through his brain and blown everything away. The edges of the lockers looked clean and sharp. He could focus intensely on the terry loops of his towel, the dark patches where water was drying off the cement floor. He avoided looking at the naked and half-dressed jocks around him. The intensity he was feeling could easily be misunderstood. He wouldn't look a dog in the eye right now, for fear of starting something.

"Hey, Johnson! Goin' out for ski team?"

Phillip stepped into the bare, echoing shower, turned the water full on, and shouted, "Blah!"

"Really?" said the voice. "That's great!"

□   □   □

The study hall teacher found the note from the office authorizing Phillip to leave and opened her attendance book. He watched her pencil make a tiny mark in a tiny square. Back of that square was a long line of *A*'s—*A* for absent.

"You've missed this study hall quite a lot in the past weeks," she said.

"Yes," said Phillip.

"Well, you're marked down. You'd better go, or you'll be late."

How long could he keep slipping through the cracks? he wondered, striding down the hall toward the office. Was this the end? He wasn't afraid. Everyone he met in the hall looked short and wimpy. Even Mr. Peabody, behind his desk, seemed like nothing he couldn't handle. Mr. Peabody waved him politely toward a chair, and he sat down. He felt as hungry as a wolf.

"Hello, Phil, how are you today?"

The blandness of the question made Phillip want to laugh. He felt like a bottle rocket going off.

"Okay."

"Good, that's good." Mr. Peabody picked up a thin manila folder from his desktop, bounced it lightly on his fingers, put it back down. "Do you like your classes here? Are you finding them any more difficult than at your previous school?"

Phillip shook his head, letting that stand as answer to both questions.

"You've, ah, you've made friends with Kris." Mr. Peabody paused for a response but didn't get one. "She's an . . . unusual . . . girl."

"Mmm." Phillip wasn't forgetting that Kris's father taught here. Anything he said about her would travel to her father like lightning.

"Well," said Mr. Peabody, abandoning the attempt to make casual conversation. "I asked to see you because . . ." He opened the file and paused, apparently seeking words. Phillip straightened slightly in his chair and, as he had hoped, was able to see over the box of tissues and the picture frames on the desk. The sheet of paper Mr. Peabody was looking at had been freshly run off on the school's tired copier. Phillip could even smell the ink. He couldn't make out a word of the short handwritten paragraph, but about halfway down he saw the sun sign.

Stunned, he leaned back in his chair and watched Mr. Peabody's bland face.

"Phillip," said Mr. Peabody, and paused again with lips closed, weighing and measuring his words before he doled them out. "Phillip, do you know what the leading cause of death is for young men in your age-group?"

"No."

"Well, it's . . . suicide." He looked at Phillip over the top of his glasses. The expression made him look at once sharp and kindly, like a television doctor. Phillip waited for what would come next, but Mr. Peabody continued to look at him.

"And?" said Phillip finally.

Mr. Peabody let out a long sigh through his nose, as if repressing irritation. He looked down at the paper again.

"Well, I . . . won't conceal from you that what you've written for this assignment disturbed Mrs. LeFevre quite a bit. Knowing what we do about your situation at home . . . well, taken by and large, this is a pretty negative statement about life, isn't it?"

She freaked! Phillip could hardly help smiling. "I don't know," he said when it became apparent that Mr. Peabody was waiting for an answer.

Mr. Peabody looked dubious. "Have you ever had suicidal thoughts?" he asked. "Have you ever thought that killing yourself would solve all your problems?"

"Is that a suggestion, sir?"

Mistake, he thought instantly, but he hadn't been able to help it. He watched Mr. Peabody master his annoyance and go into the kindly, piercing-stare routine again.

Oh, what the hell! "Yes," he said.

"Well, have you been thinking about it the last few days in particular?"

Phillip decided not to answer. Mr. Peabody flicked the Look at him.

"You realize, Phillip, that death is permanent?"

Suddenly it was getting to him. His joyous, undirected energy turned hot in his throat. I kill greyhounds twice a week, he thought, and my father is hooked to an oxygen tank. What the hell do you *think*?

"There's nothing romantic about it," Mr. Peabody

went on. "People your age often romanticize things like death and . . . so on." He glanced at the paper fleetingly. "But really it's messy and ugly and leaves an awful lot of hurt behind—"

"I know all about death," Phillip said.

"Do you? Well . . ." Mr. Peabody flipped to the second sheet in the folder, glanced at it briefly. "You know, in your situation it's no wonder you're feeling pressures. You could get free counseling after school, to help you deal with all this—"

"I have a job." Phillip stood up. "Can I go now?"

Mr. Peabody looked at him over the glasses. "I'd rather you stayed a few minutes longer, Phillip."

Phillip thought a couple of obscenities at the man, shoved his hands in his pockets, and waited.

"What I'd like to say to you, Phillip, is that you're not alone. Anytime you need to talk you can come in here—interrupt me, if need be, or see Mrs. Gilman or anyone here in the front office. We'd all be happy to listen to you." He glanced at the short page again. "You know, life is full of good things, Phillip. There's always good to balance out the bad, if only you wait."

Phillip squeezed his eyes shut. If he'd had a knife in his pocket, he'd have cut his own throat right here, just for the look on Mr. Peabody's face. He supposed he'd survive long enough for that satisfaction to register on his darkening brain. Failing that, he waited, managing not to comprehend another word until he heard, "You can go now."

The bell had not yet rung for the last class. Phillip walked straight out the nearest door.

□   □   □

Today it was Aunt Mil who picked him up.

He'd had no intention of getting a ride. He hardly knew where he was going, he was in such a rage. But within minutes a VW passed him and pulled over to the side of the road, and by the time he reached it she had picked up the mail from the passenger seat and put it in the back.

"Get in! Where are you going?"

"Work."

She had a tiny stick-on digital clock on the dashboard. He saw her glance toward it and press her lips thin.

Don't say it! he warned, internally but with considerable violence.

"You must be very early," she said. "Are you skipping school?"

"Yes," said Phillip crisply.

She glanced at the clock again. "In that case let's go get a hamburger. That woman you work for is no fool. You may as well not make extra trouble for yourself."

Extra trouble? You're trouble enough for me, lady, he thought, keeping his face toward the window.

She took him to a diner in the mall opposite the clinic and got a booth beside the front window. Phillip looked out at the cars.

She ordered and then sat looking at him, absently navigating the ice cubes in her water glass with one finger. He could hear them clink. At last she said, "You look well, Phillip."

His head jerked around, despite all efforts at coolness, and he met her eyes.

"I mean it. You look particularly alive. Skipping school agrees with you."

He wasn't going to answer that, but she was right.

"Let me set your mind at ease," she said. "I won't interfere. I won't even pick you up again, unless you stick your thumb out."

He didn't feel grateful yet, only wary. "Why not?"

Slowly and thoughtfully she dried her finger on her napkin and then started playing with the ice cubes again, never taking her eyes from him.

"Because," she said at last, "I think you know what you're doing."

In spite of himself, Phillip raised his eyebrows. Knew what he was doing?

Aunt Mil responded with a brief, sardonic smile. "What most people forget," she said, "is that school is supposed to be for learning. I don't think you're in a fit state to learn algebra and grammar right now."

"No, I've just been told I'm about to kill myself!" said Phillip. The words came out hotly and of their own accord.

Aunt Mil's clear, steely eyes studied him. "You surprise me," she said, sounding completely unsurprisable. "Who told you this?"

"Peabody," said Phillip. "Guidance."

"Guidance," said Aunt Mil. Her mouth curved down in the sour smile he liked. "And what inducement did this—Guidance—offer for staying alive?"

"He said death was permanent," said Phillip solemnly.

"I should think that was precisely the attraction," said Aunt Mil. "Well, eat your hamburger. If you're going to kill yourself, you'll need to keep up your strength!" Then she looked down and made a rueful face. "It isn't right of me to laugh. Horrible job, trying to counsel five hundred people you don't know the first thing about. He was wrong, I take it?"

"Yes," said Phillip. He was starving, suddenly, and maybe that was why he felt so strange and light-headed. He took a big bite of hamburger—and at that moment, just when he was neutralized and helpless, Aunt Mil asked, "How is your father?"

The mouthful of hamburger seemed impossibly large. Phillip chewed and swallowed at it desperately. Aunt Mil watched him but didn't apologize. She was not about to let him off the hook.

"I don't know," he said.

"Like to meet him someday." She transferred a fraction of attention to her milk shake. "I have a terminal illness, too, you know. It's called old age."

"Oh," was the most Phillip could manage.

"Would he like a visitor sometime?"

"I don't know," Phillip had to say again, and he thought of their living room, with its wall-to-wall carpet and stuffy air, the television murmuring, the duck pillows. The idea of Aunt Mil there seemed preposterous and dangerous. But he didn't know what to say that might discourage her or even if that was right. Maybe his father *would* like company. He used to be sociable—not a talker, but an enjoyer of other people, a watcher and a smiler.

"Ask him, and let me know," said Aunt Mil.

Phillip heard it more as a command than a request, and by now he was too confused to know how to respond. He managed a nod, which seemed to satisfy her for the moment.

CHAPTER SIXTEEN

He went across to the clinic and must have worked competently, because no one complained. Then home, where everything was again the same as every other night. He almost didn't mind. It was stifling, yet safe, to sit at the table with his mother and tell her that school had been "fine." Did the school call parents when they thought a student was a suicide risk? Or had it decided his parents were driving him to it, and to tell them might only make things worse? His mother knew nothing. Her eyes strained, as usual, to see the future.

After supper he went into the living room, and seeing his father in the chair, supper cooling beside him, he remembered Aunt Mil's command. He opened his mouth and found his breath pushing against a block deep in his throat.

Try again. "Dad?" The word felt strange in his mouth. He was embarrassed. When had he last spoken directly to his father?

"Dad?"

"Hmm?" His father almost glanced toward him, but something on the television caught his attention. He looked intently for a moment. Then his hand groped for the remote control. He punched the volume button three times. Suddenly the television was shouting.

". . . late victim of the farm crisis. Like almost all his neighbors, John Watson went heavily into debt to buy more land and then to buy the big equipment necessary to farm it. Though he was a good farmer by all accounts, a combination of rising interest rates and falling land value, erratic crop prices, and finally drought brought his farm to bankruptcy. Two days before his farm was to be brought under the hammer, John Watson, forty-two years old, shot himself to death. He leaves a wife and two teenage sons."

Phillip flinched from the theatrical note in the announcer's voice. The father of one of his friends had committed suicide. He knew that first there was shock, spreading a chill down your back that no wood stove or heavy coat, or even someone's arm around you, could warm up. Later it was a story told wide-eyed, in hushed voices: "I heard he . . ." "Did you

know that . . ." Mostly, it was just reality—immedi-
ate, new reality. Much was changed, but there were
still the chores, and what you had planned to do
yesterday still needed doing. The auction had to go
on, even if the man was dead. The wife had to go
on, and so did the children, forever bearing this cold,
new burden. Life could just get to be too much for
someone, but that shouldn't put the thrill of drama
in a TV announcer's voice.

Suddenly he noticed that his father's mouth was
stretched and his lips pulled in, desperately holding
something back. His eyes glittered, and he seemed to
be shaking.

His father had cried at the other farmer's funeral, like
this, almost managing to hold it back. Instinctively
Phillip looked toward the doorway, but his mother was
in the kitchen washing dishes.

"Dad?" He should get up off the couch.

"I was careful," his father said. The tears spilled over.
"I never got in debt. I didn't get too big. Thought ahead,
used my good sense. I *still* lost the farm." The tears
reached the oxygen tube, checked there, and spread
along it. "All those other guys . . . disinherited their
kids. I wasn't going to—" He coughed, and Phillip's
mother came in.

"Carl, what are you—*Carl*! What's the matter?" She
rushed to put her arms around him, and Phillip waited
numbly for his father's answer. Nothing came, but the
TV went on talking about the farm crisis until his
mother pushed the off button.

"Carl, never mind that! It's *over*. You have to save

your strength now and just think about getting better. Carl—"

Phillip got up, put on his jacket, and went out. He had never dreamed it was the farm his father was thinking of, sitting in that chair from morning till night. It was life he was regretting, youth, health. But of course, it had to be more concrete than that. It must be the farrowing, the squeal of little piglets, the smell of chopped corn. Cutting wood on cold autumn days. Finding new kittens in the barn. It must be the secure past, the work, and the future. And himself. His father must have imagined he knew what his son's future was, *where* it was. It wasn't true. Phillip had known for years that he would never be a hog farmer. But that wasn't what his father knew.

The night was cold, a mist blurring the air around the streetlights. Phillip looked up and couldn't see the sky and suddenly was pierced with longing for real dark. The sky above the gray house would be inky black, the texture of velvet. The light wind that here swirled the orange-tinted mist there would clack the bare branches and rustle the leaves. Cold and alone, he would sit on the doorstep and let his thoughts go by.

Impossible. Soon, in the warm living room, his mother would have smothered his father's grief and would look around for Phillip. Soon after that he must reappear.

His restless legs had taken him toward the playground. Now he heard small noises, and then, under the streetlights, he saw Kris.

Her back was to him, and she was throwing a ball, far out into the dim place between streetlights. As the

ball flew, so did a shadow beneath it: Diana, leaving
Kris's side with a wild scratch of claws in the hard dirt.
A bounce, a scrabble, and then she reappeared, racing
straight to Kris. She swaggered and teased for a moment. Then Kris got the ball in one hand and Diana's
collar in the other and released both winging into the
shadow again.

On her way back with the ball, Diana sensed Phillip.
She stopped, staring straight at him with one front paw
raised. Kris stepped to her side and also stared, and with
her mistress's hand on her neck, Diana was encouraged
to a muffled whoof, lips puffing out around the ball in
her teeth.

Phillip stepped forward, and Kris visibly relaxed.
"Phillip."

"Hi." He took a breath to say something flippant. But
his heart was black and heavy in his chest, and suddenly he couldn't speak. He put his hand on Diana's
head. After a moment she nudged his hip, offering the
slimy tennis ball. Mechanically Phillip took it. Kris
watched him soberly.

"Let's go sit on the swings," she said at last.

It was years since Phillip had sat on a swing. They
were closer to the ground than he remembered. Gently
he pushed himself off, in a small arc. Kris established
an opposite and exactly symmetrical arc, so that they
crossed just in the middle. Diana lay on the ground next
to her green ball, chin on paws, and watched disapprov-
ingly.

"When I was really little," Kris said, after a while,

"my father used to bring me here and push me. It seemed huge."

"You've lived here all your life?"

She snorted, Aunt Mil-like. "Doesn't seem old enough for a person's whole life, does it?"

"No."

"I remember when my hand wouldn't go all the way around the chains." Suddenly she kicked dirt, hard, and shot way back, out of sync. Her voice rose. "I remember when Victor Nugent went all the way around the top bar. They had to come with a ladder to unwrap the chains."

"He didn't fall?"

"*No*," Kris shouted. She was shooting higher and higher. To Phillip, who had stopped to watch, she looked about even with the bar at the top of her swing.

"Well, don't *you!*"

"Why not? You think a girl couldn't do it? *Swing!*"

Diana rose and expressed her concern with a grave whoof.

"You're scaring Diana."

"Scaring you, too!" But she slowed down, and Phillip started again, accelerating until they were swinging in tandem.

"Are you all right, Phillip?"

"No." He let the word out quickly and shut his mouth against the emotion that wanted to follow.

Right now he was thinking of the tire swing in front of the farmhouse, remembering its deliciously lazy round arc and how you could kick off the tree trunk once you got going hard enough. He remembered his father lifting him into it, saw his own skinny little legs swallowed by the enormous hole, felt the sunshine, smelled the hogs. . . .

"We used to have a tire swing."

"I always wanted one," said Kris. "Dad said it would make the place look like a junkyard." She brought her swing to a stop and began to turn herself and the seat around, twisting the chain. When they were as tight as they could be, she let go, twirling rapidly. Diana looked away, as if it were more than she could bear to watch.

When she had come to a stop once more, head swaying, Kris asked, "Do you want to go back there?"

"Can't."

"I mean, would you? You said once that it was ugly, and it stank."

Maybe it would steady him to think of that—the dark side of the farm, things he used to hate. He explored it cautiously, but it only added to the blackness and hurt in his chest.

"It's the hogs," he said. "You have to try not to look at them, because they're so smart, and their skin's the same color as ours. It's—it was just scary, if you got to thinking." His father's brow, dripping sweat as he corralled a loose hog, a hog that had made a break for freedom . . .

"Why didn't you become a vegetarian?"

You would have, he thought. "Everything was alive once—even plants."

"Animal rights people say farming is exploiting the animals."

Yes, thought Phillip. But he was no longer implicated. He decided to turn the tables.

"Why aren't *you* an animal rights person?"

"I don't believe in rights. I don't know what a right is." She smiled grimly. "I only know what's wrong."

"And it's not wrong to eat animals?"

"Animals eat animals. Why shouldn't I?"

"You expect more from people. You said so once."

"Hey, the guy heard something I said! Maybe there's somebody in there after all!" She wound herself up and twirled again.

Phillip knew he probably deserved that, but he didn't like it. He got up from the swing. "I better get back."

Kris stopped herself in mid-twirl and stood up. Her eyes rolled up, and she grabbed him to steady herself. "Wait—I'll walk you home."

But they weren't walking yet. Did she expect him to put his arms around her? He should want to. He loved Kris, really, and liked the way she looked, and he was a teenage guy. Shouldn't his hormones be the most important thing in the world to him right now?

Diana whined jealously. Kris laughed and let him go. They shoved their hands in their pockets and turned toward the street. Diana paced soberly between them.

After a moment he sensed Kris looking at him. She was wondering, he knew, and not daring to ask. And what *could* she ask? She knew about his father; she, of all people, did not expect him to be a normal, happy person. Yet they had never talked about it. It was impossible to discuss, a looming bulk in the back of his mind, shadowing everything. The bulk had moved closer tonight, that was all, and he couldn't tell her that. He wished they could go back to the playground, ride the teeter-totter and twirl the old wooden merry-go-round, just laugh and not talk.

"Will your dog mind if we hold hands?"

She was startled and almost stopped walking. He was startled himself, but yes, it was what he wanted. He half drew his hand from his pocket, watching to see if she would do the same. Slowly she did. Cold from the swing chains, their hands clasped above Diana's back. Without looking at each other, they walked down the street to his house.

What next? Phillip wondered, as his own roof came into view in the murky streetlight. If this were television, they would pause and kiss gently. Someday he would want to. Now he wanted only support—the cold, strong hand that held his, or at most, a hug.

What did Kris want?

But the yard light was on, and his mother stood at the door, looking anxiously out. As soon as she saw him, she put her hand to the latch, and his hand and Kris's instantly parted.

"See ya," said Kris, and vanished.

"Phillip, where have you *been*?" cried his mother, opening the door. Thea appeared from the shadows and zipped past her into the house.

"Went for a walk," said Phillip, knowing that the answer didn't matter. What mattered to his mother was holding things still, keeping everyone *here*, and *stable*, for as long as she could.

"I'm gonna take a shower," he said, but passed

through the living room briefly, pretending to look for something. The television was off, but his father sat in the chair as usual, tidied back into his habitual expression. Only it didn't seem quite as firm to Phillip. Something had moved, and though it had been set in place again, like a stone put back on a tumbling wall, the cement of lichen and old leaves was gone.

□ □ □

He was in the kitchen later, making a cup of hot milk, when the phone rang.

His mother came around the corner, glancing at the clock and then at Phillip, her eyes full of conjecture. It was nine forty-five. Not many people called that late.

"Hello? ... Oh, Carrie! Hi, honey." The anxiety dropped from her face and then came back full force. "*What*? He *what*?"

Derek! thought Phillip, jerking the pan and slopping milk on the burner. It smoked and stank. There was a skin on top. He poured it down the sink and stood watching his mother's face, which was full of astonishment and distress.

"Oh, *honey*! Sweetheart, just forget about him. He isn't worth a single tear ... oh, *sweetie*!"

"What did he do?" Phillip asked roughly. A sound from the living room; then his father stood in the doorway. He looked taller, his shoulders thrown back, his chest rising and falling with his angry breath. Phillip's mother shook her head helplessly at them, listening into the phone. Phillip had the impression that all she could hear was crying.

"What, darling? . . . Yes? . . . Listen, blow your nose, and calm down, and tell me. . . . Yes, all right, run and get one. Of course, I'll wait." Now she took the phone from her ear and looked at her husband and Phillip. "She says he *dumped* her!"

"Tell her congratulations!" Phillip said. His mother only looked at him, in unchanged shock, until Carrie's voice on the phone reclaimed her.

Now for a long time she said only, "Uh-huh. Uh-huh. Uh-huh." Phillip roamed restlessly around the kitchen, waiting for a significant word to fall. He thought passionately about Derek, and the things he wanted to do to Derek.

Suddenly his mother stopped making any sound at all. Phillip wasn't even sure she was breathing. She gripped the receiver and listened hard, mouth half-open. Her eyes looked frightened and miles away.

"But how can I leave your dad all alone?" she asked finally.

Phillip met his father's eyes. He was startled at their brilliance. Alone?

"Oh, honey, I don't see how . . . I know, but—" She covered the mouthpiece with her hand and looked at them. "She wants me to go *out* there!"

"Go," his father said.

"But, Carl—"

"Go on. We'll hold the fort."

She looked helplessly around her kitchen: spotless, gleaming, replete with duck needlepoints and duck potholders. Then she closed her eyes briefly.

"All right. I'll come. Is your roommate there this

weekend? . . . Then I'll pick you up around ten-thirty or eleven, and we'll run up to Aunt Vivian's. Now, Carrie, I want you to try and sleep, but if you can't, get up and do homework, so you won't have *that* to worry about. And make some nice hot tea, and don't cry any more than you have to. Promise? . . . Yes, Daddy's right here, and so is Phillip." She held the phone out to her husband.

Carl Johnson didn't communicate in words. It was the hands, squeezing your shoulder or skimming a cuff across the top of your head. It was the eyes.

"Hi, baby," he said, and listened for a while. "I wish you were here. . . . Yeah, we'll be all right. . . . Yeah. . . . No. . . . No." He listened a moment more and then said softly, "Yeah, I love you, too. . . . Yeah. . . . Here." He gave the phone to Phillip.

"Hi, Phlip?" Her voice was thick and shaky.

"Hi, Care. You okay?"

"No," she said, with a choke. "Actually, no, I'm not okay. I just wanted to tell you that you were right."

Phillip winced. "You don't have to say that!" Typical Carrie!

"No, I want to. All it took was—I just started thinking more about *my* problems. Like you said, I was his mirror, and when he stopped seeing himself, he just looked for another one."

"He's a shit!"

"No, he's just . . . had a really hard life. . . ."

"And you haven't?"

"Not till now, no." He could hear a sound almost like panting; she was starting to cry again.

"*Hey*! Remember what Mom said?"

Sniff. "Can I talk to her again?"

"Sure. Um . . . take care, all right?" He handed the phone back to his mother.

They were a long time saying good-bye. Phillip and his father drifted back into the living room, waiting.

At last she put down the receiver and came around the corner. "Oh, my! I never would have dreamed . . . He seemed like . . ." She was unable to finish, unable to reconstruct what Derek had seemed like.

Phillip's father sat down in his chair again.

"Oh, my goodness. Well, Phillip, I'm going to write you out a list of phone numbers. . . ."

A list of phone numbers, prominent among them doctors, emergency rooms, and ambulance services. A list of his father's medicines. A list of where food was kept . . .

"I know where all the food is," Phillip said. But a list was made, and also cooking instructions. In desperation—as all the lists and instructions were also being given verbally—Phillip went to bed.

□   □   □

He would be alone with his father.

He couldn't imagine what they might say to each other. His mother brokered whatever small conversations they now had, so eager for each word that fell from her husband's lips that Phillip knew he always had to share. Did they have anything to say to each other? And would they say it? The possibility of talking worried him as much as the possibility of not talking.

He sat up. Despite his day—oh, God, his *day*! How many miles had he walked?—his body would not be still. Nothing could wear him out anymore. All his extra walking only made him fitter.

He opened his door. Instantly his mother appeared at the end of the hall. He went into the bathroom.

"Phillip, am I making too much noise for you?" she asked at the door.

"No."

"I'm just making up a couple of things for you two to eat." She started to tell him what. Phillip stifled a groan, slipped out of his pajamas, and got into the shower. He turned it on very hot.

"Phillip?" Now she was *in* the bathroom! "Why are you taking another shower? You had one earlier. . . ."

Phillip made a violent grimace, actually hurting some jaw muscles. "I can't sleep!"

"Oh. Well . . ." After a moment he heard the door shut.

CHAPTER SEVENTEEN

Early in the morning she drove away. The sky was just lightening, and the air was very cold, with a fresh, wet feel. Snow coming, Phillip thought.

He and his father were up early to say good-bye. His mother looked anxious and faraway but didn't say much. She gave each of them a long hug, and Phillip carried her overnight case out to the car. She sat with the driver's door open for a few minutes, letting the engine warm up a little.

"He should have plenty of oxygen till I get back," she said suddenly, "but if not, call the hospital. They'll tell you how to have some delivered." She looked up into his face. "I'm counting on you, Phillip."

"Mmm," said Phillip. In fact, she was not counting on him at all. She was doing her best not to have to, with her lists and her instructions. Phillip didn't blame her. He felt himself that he could be counted on for the essentials, but not to cover the full extent of her anxieties.

"Drive safe," he said.

"I will." She closed the door and shifted the car into reverse. Phillip stood back and watched her go, already looking serious and competent in the precise economy of her turn. As she disappeared, he saw her in his mind's eye, streaming down the gray highways, wide-eyed and alert. This was the woman who mastered the computer by reading the manuals; the woman who could kill a chicken and gut it, though she cried if a weasel did the same; the woman who had engineered the move here, to a part of the country where they had no relatives, so no one would be always pitying them. He imagined her opening the window partway, pressing her foot on the accelerator to an efficient but illegal speed, her men and her home slipping behind her with the miles.

When he went back inside, the house felt empty, with a sort of vibration on the air. He didn't know what to do next.

His father sat at the table, stirring a cup of coffee. Phillip looked at him obliquely and caught the tail end of a slanting glance. "What's the weather look like out there?"

"Cold. Might snow."

"She'll be okay, though. Your mother."

"Yeah."

His father coughed and took a sip of coffee. "Guess I'll lie down. . . ." He looked grayish, and he grunted with each exhalation, grunted as he pushed himself up from the table. Mornings were hard for him.

A couple of hours later Phillip had a second breakfast, and in the middle of it his father woke up. The coughing was horrible—both pitiful and disgusting. Phillip usually avoided hearing it, being on his way to school weekdays and either outdoors or buried in his room with headphones on weekend mornings. He hated being the kind of person who put on headphones first thing in the morning, and he thought he should be stronger. But he left his breakfast and went outside, pretending to check the mailbox. When he came back inside, it was over, and his father was at the coffeemaker, pouring himself a cup. He inhaled the steam for a moment, then poured in the cream and looked over at Phillip.

"What are your plans?"

"Aah . . ." said Phillip, blankly. People never asked him that. He hardly ever made plans anyway.

"Did she say—your mother—that you shouldn't leave the house?"

Had she? It had been implied in every instruction, but perhaps not actually said.

"'Cause—" Carl Johnson took another sip of coffee. "I haven't been alone for . . . six months, and if . . . you've got stuff to do, I want you to do it. Okay?"

"Okay," Phillip said. His voice sounded thin and young to him. He wished he'd put more breath into it.

"Couple things first. Find me a lawn chair. I want to sit out awhile."

"It's cold," Phillip said.

His father's face twisted in an unusual expression of bitterness. "What am I going to do? Get sick?"

Phillip took a deep, openmouthed breath. "And the other thing?"

"Huh?"

"You wanted a couple things?" This was hard labor, prying words out of his father, and the man was unusually talkative this morning.

"Oh." His father turned and looked through the doorway into the living room. "Put those . . . goddamned pillows in a closet somewhere. And . . . take 'em out tomorrow. Make *sure!"*

Phillip gathered up an armful of pillows and dropped them into the hall closet where the winter coats were kept. Some of the ducks and geese were cute, and some were actually beautiful. He hoped they wouldn't get dirty on the closet floor, but of course, the closet floor was very clean.

When he left, his father was leaning back into the corner of the couch, coffee mug between his hands, looking at the cold white sky through the picture window.

□   □   □

So, at ten o'clock, Phillip found himself out on the road. His day was his own, whether he liked it or not.

One good thing—on his hip, buckled to his belt, a small saucepan and a tin cup bounced up and down. In his pocket were some packages of instant cocoa. With his mother out of the house, he'd been able to liberate these items.

He was almost to the high school when he heard the first shot. Only then did he remember: first day of deer season.

He looked down at himself. His barn jacket and his jeans were dulled blue denim. His sweater was brown. Might as well paint a white tail on his butt!

He braked, wondering if he should turn back, go to the mall and buy an orange vest. It seemed a long way to go, for something he didn't really want.

Then he remembered the little store he'd found the day that he got lost.

□ □ □

The store was bustling with activity, people buying ammo and talking ammo, and stalking, and great shots they had made or almost made. A guy with a newly killed deer in the back of his pickup stopped to get his gas tank topped off and to brag. A girl whom Phillip had seen at school was buying milk, and a couple of people got lottery tickets.

Phillip walked up and down the four aisles, trying to convince himself that he couldn't see a single flash of orange. Surely all stores like this carried hunting vests or at least orange knit hats. Didn't they? On a day like this he could really appreciate one of those hats.

He picked up a can of tomato soup and went up to the counter to ask, something that was normally against his principles. As he stood behind a woman buying cigarettes and lottery tickets, he spotted his first flash of red in the whole store—a cotton bandanna hung on the wall behind the storekeeper's head.

"How much are the handkerchiefs?" he asked when it was his turn.

"Dollar."

"I'll take . . ." He paused and checked his pockets. "Five. I'll put the soup back."

"Can't eat a bandanna, kid," the man said, winking at the next person in line. But he brought out five new bandannas, neatly folded, and when Phillip couldn't find enough change to pay the sales tax, the man shooed him away. "I'll get it from the next guy!" Wink.

Phillip put the soup back on the shelf, only briefly giving any thought to stealing it. He had no can opener anyway, and he'd probably just lose it all if he chopped the can open with the hatchet.

At the edge of the woods he tied the bandannas on himself, making a skimpy vest which covered only the upper third of his chest. He blushed even to think of a hunter seeing him and had to remind himself that to be brought low by a bullet, all for the sake of vanity, would be even more ridiculous. But he walked quickly, eager for the shelter of the gray house.

The kittens weren't around. Of course, on a morning like this, they had to disappear. He called a couple of times, then kept himself busy laying a fire and getting his pan of water. When he went to the door again, ready to take to the woods and start calling in spite of the potential embarrassment, they were coming around the corner, blinking. They must have been asleep in the foundation.

"Hi, guys!" He picked them up. One squeaked in faint protest. The other looked straight into his eyes, in a drowsy, intimate way.

"Why don't you have names?" he asked them. The sleepy one put a soft paw to his lips, then stretched against him and yawned widely. "Hi," he said to it again.

The other one struggled out of his arms, landed on the floor with a solid thump, and stretched. The stretch was audible, a distinct shudder on the air. Phillip had always known that you could hear a cat stretch, but for the first time it struck him as strange. What was he actually hearing? The muscles? The hairs, shivering against one another?

Everything was strange. He fed the kittens, lit his fire, and put the pan of water on to heat. As the tiny flames and smoke curls twined up through the branches, the hurt came out where he could see it.

He was a fool, he told himself, and selfish. He had imagined his father had something to say to him that he could say to no one else.

It was true. What his father had to say was, "I want to be alone."

Phillip tried to feel honored by this. He knew it *was* an honor. Masks were slipping. They were all starting to say true things to one another, and this is what his father said to *him*. Him, and no one else. "I want to be alone. You are the one I can ask. You are the one who is strong enough."

Yet his heart swelled with hurt, and though he told himself that he was doing a good thing, that he was brave and strong and generous, that was only a thin voice speaking from beyond the edge. Hurt ballooned bigger in his chest with every breath. He took a kitten on his lap, hoping that might help, and stared at the flames for a long time, until the fire had burned down to a heap of gray ashes, and it was time to go home.

□   □   □

When Phillip swooped into the driveway, the

kitchen door was open. The side door of the garage was open, too, and between the two, down the steps and across the concrete pad, ran the oxygen line. It wasn't moving.

"Dad?" Phillip dropped his bike in the driveway. "Dad?"

The line stirred. Now he saw Thea, sitting gravely at the top of the steps. As the line moved, she regarded it for a moment and then softly poked it with her paw.

His father was standing in the garage doorway. He glanced around as Phillip came in, his face slightly strange, like the face of a person you haven't seen for a couple of months.

"Um . . ." said Phillip. "Ah, it's pretty cold out here. Don't you think . . ." His words made no contact and thinned out into nothingness.

His father turned slightly, looking into the far back corner of the garage. His shoulders seemed to sag. Finally he said, in a soft, husky voice, "Phillip, what the hell can I *do*?"

It was the kind of question Phillip's mind went blank on. What can I *do*? About what? In the still garage he could hear his father's breathing. A number of horrible possibilities presented themselves, but he felt entirely bereft of words.

"There's nothing to *do*," his father said. He turned now to Phillip, lifting his big, empty hands in a way that suddenly made everything clearer. "I wanted to think, but . . . I can't think if I'm not *doing* anything."

Of course, Phillip thought, remembering his own need, in all the beautiful solitude of the gray house, to do some work and thinking of the two armfuls of duck pillows in the closet.

But everything here was finished and put away. In the house everything was cleaned, polished, new.

"I don't know, but come inside. You'll catch cold."

His father didn't move. "I'll get pneumonia. You know what they . . . used to call pneumonia, Phillip? The old man's friend."

"Come *on!*"

After a long moment his father turned and heavily climbed the steps. The oxygen cord dragged behind, and Thea followed, poking it. Phillip pushed it the last couple of inches with his toe and closed the door. His father stood in the kitchen now, hands at his sides, gazing blankly at the spotless countertop.

"You could sharpen the splitting hammer and the wedges," Phillip offered.

"Hmm? Oh . . ." His father looked around, in vague interest. It was enough. Phillip went back to the garage.

The hammer and wedges were still in the grain bag, where he'd left them. He rummaged through the toolbox and found the file, then brought them inside, where his father had already spread a newspaper on the table.

"How about the ax?" he asked, sitting down.

"Aah . . ." said Phillip.

His father looked up.

"I've got it," Phillip said. "Out in the woods." His father's face remained calmly curious, unthreatening, and essentially unreadable. "Hatchet, too," Phillip said.

"They need sharpening?"

"Well, yeah, I s'pose they might, by now. I'll—" His father terminated the babble by looking down again and picking up the file.

"Why don't you bring in the chain saw, too?" he suggested after a minute. "Can't remember how we left it."

"Okay." Phillip went out the door again. The air looked strange, like water with clear oil swirled through it, the air of unreality. His father would never use the chain saw again, never raise the splitting hammer over his head and swing it down on a chunk of wood. But to sharpen these tools was useful work, the last work he would do with them. . . . It was all too bewildering for tears. He picked up the heavy chain saw and the little tool kit that went with it and carried them inside.

"Thanks," his father said.

"Um . . . you had lunch?"

"Don't want any."

Phillip stood a moment, watching his father stroke the file over a wedge, straightening its curled and crumpled edge. "So . . . you want me to leave?"

His father looked up again. His eyes seemed unfocused. This must be very strange to him, too. Never mind the fear and the anger at being wrenched away from everything. At some deep level it was all just strange. Too strange for the conventional emotions . . .

"Yes," his father said. "If you wouldn't mind."

CHAPTER EIGHTEEN

do mind, thought Phillip. He was on his bike again, moving, with no place to go.

He turned down Kris's street and went through the motions of inquiring for her at home. Of course, she was at Aunt Mil's. He and she agreed about weekends: too much opportunity for closeness with your family.

It was one thing to escape from your home and quite another to be pushed out. It was . . .

"Oh, crap!" he said aloud. The one thing his father had asked of him, since the beginning of his illness, and here he was dissolved in self-pity.

It would have been nice if his father had wanted to talk.

Well, he doesn't. He has somebody trying to talk with him twenty-four hours of the day, and he can't ask *her* to get out. For this very reason.

Still . . .

Oh, gimme a *break*!

He found himself outside Aunt Mil's picket fence, leaned his bike against it, and went up the path. His knock went unanswered, but he heard voices, and cautiously, wondering whether he should, he opened the door. "Hello?"

Kris was on her knees in the pantry, scrubbing. Hot pine cleaner smell boiled up around her. Aunt Mil stood on a chair, reaching something down from the top shelf.

They looked around at him, and Aunt Mil said, "Good! Stop right there, take off your shoes, and come take these things from me."

"These things" were glass cake and cheese covers, sherbet glasses, a punch bowl, and a small tea set, all covered with a thin film of dust.

"No, we're not having a party," Aunt Mil said. "Come here, lend me your shoulder." She leaned one bony hand on him, not heavily, and stepped down from the chair. "There, Kris, I'll get this out of your way. Now that the garden's put away for the year, it's time to clean all the things I never use. Have to make work for this girl, so her father won't think she comes just for the subversive talk."

She squeezed dish soap into one half of the sink and turned on the hot water. "Do you want to wash or dry?"

Phillip realized she was speaking to him. "Uh, wash." He tested the water with one finger. Too hot. His hands were frozen to the marrow, and in very hot water they would feel as if they were splitting. He ran some cold, filled the other sink with rinse water, and plunged in his hands. They burned coldly for a few moments and turned lobster red. He started on the sherbet glasses.

They were all silent, working. The sun came out weakly, veiled by a thin overcast. Suddenly Phillip remembered Aunt Mil picking him up on the road, only yesterday. Walking out of school. Mr. Peabody.

And the playground last night, swinging and holding Kris's hand.

The air was full of the things they all knew and hadn't told, or wouldn't tell, as well as the things they

wondered. It made a pressure, which somehow accentu-
ated the quiet. With his hands in the dishwater, and the
sun pale on the fuzzy cactus over the sink, all at once
Phillip felt happy and peaceful, as if he had an untouch-
able stillness walled within his heart.

He washed the cake covers and the cheese covers. He
could see himself on their surfaces, transparent and dis-
torted, the small spontaneous smile on his face turned
to a Howdy Doody grin. He stopped smiling, but the
cake cover made him smile anyway, now a secretive
smirk. He looked up at the window.

There he was again, this time reflected accurately. He
was still transparent, though, and through himself he
could see the brown November yard and the white
picket fence.

"What do you see?" asked Aunt Mil. He realized he
had been standing still, looking, for a noticeable
amount of time.

□   □   □

After work they sat down to tea and gingersnaps and
talked about adopting greyhounds. Kris's father had
given his firm and absolute no: no fostering, no kennel
in his backyard, no more pets of any kind.

"Well, I'm not going to volunteer," Aunt Mil said.
"At my age I don't think a greyhound is what I need."

"It's all right," said Kris confidently. "I'll work it out
with Dr. Franklin. The first one will be just overnight,
so it'll be gone before he can do anything. The next one
will be longer, and before you know it, he'll be *forcing*
me to build a kennel!"

"You understand him all too well," said Aunt Mil dryly.

Then she thought of Phillip's father. He could almost hear the click as the association slid into place, and even before she spoke, even before her eyes turned toward him, he felt a thrill of alarm. But it was too late.

"Did you speak to your father, Phillip?" she asked.

A bubble of air seemed to rise in Phillip's throat. He had to swallow it before he could speak. "Um, no. Actually my—my mother's away, and . . . he wants to be alone. He hasn't been alone in six months, he said."

Her eyes sharpened on him, alarmingly. "And where does that leave you, Phillip?"

Phillip didn't know how to answer. They were both looking at him now. "I—I just went out. . . ."

"Have you been out of the house all day?"

"Um . . . no. I was back at lunchtime. . . ."

Aunt Mil closed her mouth abruptly, and it made a long, firm downward curve across her face. She looked out the window at the cold gray day. "You are always welcome here," she said, after a moment.

Phillip should say something, he knew, but he felt stuck inside. He just sat. The silence lengthened, until Kris suddenly glanced at the clock and said, "Oh, Lord, I've got to go!"

Phillip made his escape then, and they walked together. He wheeled his bike, putting it and Diana between himself and Kris. They were a whole sidewalk apart and didn't speak for a long time.

"Derek dumped Carrie," Phillip said at last. "Now he's going out with a bathroom mirror." He waited; she didn't laugh. "That's where Mom went."

"To see Carrie?"

"Yeah."

Silence again. The cold had sharpened, and a wind was blowing. Diana, with her short, thin hair, huddled miserably and shivered. She was the kind of dog that ought to have a coat, Phillip thought, and he thought out a couple of neat, witty ways to say so to Kris. But he didn't. Her profile looked stern, forbidding speech, especially anything witty and frivolous. They approached his street, the parting of ways.

"Well—" he said lightly, and at the same time Kris said, "Aunt Mil told me she picked you up. What happened, with Peabody?"

With Peabody? How did she know about Peabody? And what could he tell her?

She was staring at him, her eyes growing brighter and harder, a flush rising to her cheeks. "Thanks, Phillip," she said abruptly. "Thanks a *lot*!" And she strode off up the street, Diana trotting effortlessly alongside. Phillip stared at her, still groping for an answer, hardly able to grasp that she was gone.

□   □   □

His father sat in the living room with no lights on. He turned his head when Phillip came in. Thea was draped across his chest, fast asleep.

"You want supper?" Phillip asked.

"No. Fix some for yourself."

Phillip left the living room, as he knew he was meant to. The house felt dark and too quiet. He opened the refrigerator. All the containers, which had been so well explained to him, looked blank and sterile. He couldn't think what was in them, and after all, he wasn't hungry. He went and took a very long, very hot shower.

Then he sat on his bed and looked at a book, passed his eyes over the words, gradually easing his attention away from the wounded feeling in his own heart and the little conversations he kept making up to regain people's attention. Everyone had a fragmented and mistaken image of him. He should have explained himself better.

CHAPTER NINETEEN

When he awoke, the light was still on and he was fully dressed. He glanced at the clock. Three A.M. He didn't feel aggrieved this time. He felt exceptionally clearheaded, pleased to be awake now, when no one else was. For once he knew exactly what to do.

He got off the bed, put on a sweater, and stopped at his desk to write a note.

>Dad
>
>I couldn't sleep. Went to get the ax and hatchet for you. Back for breakfast.
>
>Phillip

He almost expected to find his father still in the chair, but snores came from his parents' bedroom. Phillip put the note on the counter, got a flashlight and his jacket, and slipped out the door, closing it softly behind him. His bike was on the breezeway. He wheeled it out to the street and mounted.

Cold. He pushed into it, watching his own shadow lengthen and diminish as he passed from one streetlight to another.

All day, explaining himself to others or hiding himself; never succeeding. Looking for himself in all those mirrors. Struggling to bring himself into focus. He felt that he had been looking for support, and now he was upright, undivided. He passed out of streetlights and into darkness, his feeble, bobbing headlight probing dimly along the yellow line. There were no cars. Every house was dark. Only an alert dog or two noticed his passing.

At last he came to the farm, also dark, swooped through the silent yard and out into the frost-rimed cornfield, feeling the immense, empty space around him. What he missed most about their own farm, and about farm country, was the emptiness. That's what farms are for, he thought, slowing, hitting a hump of manure, getting off to walk. A farm like this was the silent, open heart of the countryside. He was grateful to the unknown people who worked so hard here, perhaps thinking only of the living they were trying to make. If they could not make a living here, they should be given one, so the quiet could endure.

Somewhere ahead in the black trees he heard the fierce cry of an owl. It made a long, rounded shape on the air, reaching out across the field. His feet crunched on the frosty ground.

At the edge of the woods he left his bike and started climbing. After a few minutes he turned the flashlight off and waited, balanced lightly on the balls of his feet, until his eyes began to adjust. Then he started on again. He felt that his heart, and not his senses, guided him. He was part of the dark woods, and it was impossible for him to lose his way. The thin carpet of worn and trodden leaves seemed to come up and find his feet at every step. The trees stretched their arms along the road to guide him.

The brook was loud for a while, and then he came to the house. The roof slates gleamed slightly. His feet found the path down through the silvery weeds. He touched the door latch and remembered his dream—coming to a lonely gray house on a stormy night. Never once had he felt that the dream was a psychic event. Simply it was a part of himself, telling him what he needed. He opened the door on the greater darkness within.

He waited and eventually could see how the light came in the window: the fireplace, the cross-hatching of the kindling pile, the sharp edge of the kittens' box. He walked across the floor, hearing his own footsteps and nothing else. The leaves no longer shivered in the corners. The kittens had caught all the mice, or else they were hibernating.

The kittens were hibernating, too. He could barely see them when he peered into the dark box, and he had to explore with his hand to make sure there were two. When he touched them, they didn't stir, and their light breathing hardly lifted his hand. They were surprisingly warm, though, and he could smell, rising from them faintly, the sweet fresh-laundry smell of cats that have recently bathed. They were a luxurious presence in the barren room, amid the dead leaves and raccoon dung. Phillip crouched for a while beside them, his hand lifting and dropping with their breaths like a small boat riding the breath of the ocean. Only when his legs cramped did he rise, go outside, and sit on the cold front step.

He saw the black branches of the locust trees snaggling across the sky with bright stars caught in them. He listened to the brook and the night noises. He felt like a person who doesn't know people and doesn't miss them, a person, perhaps, who doesn't even know how to read.

Eventually the branches became clear, and the stars dimmer. The air grew gray, and a cold fog rose. Phillip went inside and filled the kittens' food dish. They were still sleeping. He slipped out the door, shut it softly, and went up the path through the tall weeds, shrugging on his vest as he went.

□   □   □

He'd forgotten the ax and hatchet, but his father was still asleep, so it didn't matter. Phillip crushed the note in one hand and dropped it in the wastebasket, then took his frozen body into the shower. He had filled the room with steam and turned himself beet red all over before he was warmed through. Then, blameless in flannel pajamas and a bathrobe, he started making breakfast. In a few minutes he heard his father stir.

He came out in his pajamas and poured a mug of coffee, stood looking out the window at the bleak backyard. He didn't speak. That wasn't as burdensome as usual to Phillip, without his mother's concern for contrast. Nor was it perfectly easy. But he kept himself quiet, and poured the batter into the waffle iron.

"Your mother called yesterday," his father said eventually.

"When?"

His father shrugged. He had never been one to dwell on unnecessary details, never one to pause in the midst of a story to decide if it had happened on a Tuesday or a Wednesday. Now he had even less breath to waste.

"Said you were out."

Phillip watched the steam curl up from the edges of the waffle iron, waiting.

"Carrie's okay," his father said, after a while. "They went to Vivian's. Viv'll look after her for us—get her on weekends, as long as she needs it."

"Good," said Phillip. Of course, Derek wasn't the only thing troubling Carrie or even the main thing. She would need help for a long time to come, and the peace of Vivian's place, with the goats and the lady companion who might be a lover, though they never wondered that aloud, would be good for her.

But what had his parents said about *him*?

His father had nothing more to offer. They ate their breakfast in almost total silence. His father ate four waffles; like his mother, Phillip found himself counting. He himself ate many more than four. Then he washed the dishes, carefully cleaned off the counter, and swept the kitchen floor. What was he supposed to do today?

He passed the living room and glanced in. His father sat in the chair. His big hands rested quietly on the arms, and he looked out the window. His eyes were clear and thoughtful; his expression was firm. Phillip felt that it didn't matter what he did. He could go out or he could stay. His father would not notice.

He took himself quietly outdoors.

His father saw him through the picture window and waved as he pushed off. Phillip waved back and accelerated, as if he were rushing off to meet someone. Out of sight of his own house he slowed down, weaving back and forth across the empty streets.

He knew what he looked like: the kids in town, teenage boys who rode bikes too small for them down the sidewalks and around and around the parking lots. They had outgrown the last bikes their parents could afford to buy them or felt like buying them, and they were a year or so too young for jobs and used cars to roar around in. Between ages, with nothing on their minds, they cruised the streets, like Phillip now. . . .

A VW passed him. Two stern female faces looked his way in surprise and disapproval. Abruptly the car pulled into the next driveway, turned around, and headed back up the street, passing him again. He received one curt nod apiece and sat up straight on his bike and gawked, almost running into a fire plug, as the VW turned into his own street.

"*Shit!*" He accelerated, shot a little wide turning into his street, and grazed someone's leafless hedge, pedaled madly. Halfway down the street he heard the unmistakable sound of a storm door shutting. Too late.

More slowly now he looped into his own yard and parked his bike in the breezeway. He heard the storm door again. Kris stood on the top step.

"You're shivering," she said, looking him over with a critical expression.

"Oh." So he was, some inside and some out. "What's going on?"

"Officially we're looking for you. Your father said you weren't home, and Aunt Mil said, 'Do you know where he is?'"

"Oh, come *on!*" said Phillip angrily. "She doesn't have a right to give him shit like that!"

"She doesn't believe in rights, either. She believes in duties, and she said she wouldn't stand by and watch you turned into a street urchin just because you seem older than you are. She's here to remind your parents—in her subtle way—that they're the adults."

"Well, Mom isn't here, and Dad—look, he needed the time, and I gave it to him, and I'm glad!"

"That's wonderful," said Kris politely. "You'd look even nobler if your nose weren't blue."

"You two think you know everything!" Annoyed beyond endurance, Phillip pushed past her into the house.

He could see what had happened. Both were still on their feet, his father running a hand through his hair, confused and helpless. The hall closet stood open, and a large armful of pillows had been dumped back on the couch. His father must have heard the car in the driveway and panicked. Aunt Mil was soothing him, pouring on the charm. Already she was being offered a cup of something and was accepting graciously and taking off her coat.

"I'll get it," Phillip said, filling the kettle.

"Oh, hello, Phillip," Aunt Mil said, on an entirely false note of surprise.

He scowled at her.

Turning away, opening the cupboard to get tea bags, he was astonished to intercept a powerful beam of authority from his father's eye. You be-*have*, his father told him silently. He also expressed surprise at Phillip's rudeness and called clearly for help. Phillip's hands fumbled, and he dropped several boxes of different kinds of tea on the counter. Kris moved silently to his side to help sort them out.

"This is what we have," Phillip said. He made every effort to lighten and politen his voice, with the result that he sounded like a car salesman.

Regally Aunt Mil made her choice. Nothing in her demeanor suggested that they had ever spoken together as equals. They were firmly old lady, boy. Phillip felt confused and hurt.

Yet this made it natural, when the tea was ready, for her and his father to retire to the living room together, Phillip and Kris to remain at the table.

Polite conversation. Aunt Mil admired a duck pillow, at the same time covertly straightening the jumble.

"My wife's work."

"Beautiful." Her eyes traveled around the room. Phillip saw them check as they crossed the oxygen cord, drawing its line across the green carpet, check, and return.

"Are you permanently tied to that thing?"

"Yes," said Phillip's father. He didn't seem to be shocked, as Phillip was. They tried never to mention the cord among themselves, but of course, his father must be always thinking of it.

"Are you restricted to the house then?"

"No. I have portable tanks. They tell me I can—do whatever I feel like. Don't feel like much, though."

"Well, of course not!" snapped Aunt Mil. "There's nothing to do. Whatever possessed you to move to a place like this?"

Phillip's father leaned back in his chair and looked her over, with an expression that Phillip hadn't seen on his face in a long time. A politician stumping for votes, a pesticide salesman, the lady president of the local bird-watchers' society used to provoke it: a compound of amusement and wariness.

"We mainly wanted to . . . get out of range of our relatives," he said. "And . . . someplace that wouldn't be much . . . trouble to run."

"So you could spend all your time thinking about your condition!"

"That has been the result."

Amusement was winning. He still held himself back, protected, but a smile was struggling to control the corner of his mouth.

"You probably think I'm a terrible old woman," said Aunt Mil. "But the odds are you won't die a day sooner than I will, so we may as well discuss it openly!"

"In that case, ma'am, I'll just point out, I'm a little younger than you are."

The corners of her mouth twitched as she nearly smiled. "Yes," she said. "I've had more time."

"And," said Phillip's father, "I've been . . . sitting here, thinking of the . . . time *I* had, and the time I . . . won't have. And missing this time."

Neither of them glanced toward the kitchen, but Phillip knew that he had been referred to.

"You ought to have a little farm," said Aunt Mil.

Phillip's father shook his head. "No. What I . . . have coming to me is . . . bad. She won't need . . . extra work."

"How soon?" asked Aunt Mil.

Phillip wanted to look away from his father's face but couldn't, and he was surprised that his father's expression did not change. Answering the question seemed easy for him. He seemed glad to.

"A couple years, they say. Maybe more. Maybe less. They really don't know."

Phillip hadn't known either. Two years. Part of him relaxed. Part of him froze in dread.

"But then," said Aunt Mil, "you're in exactly the same position as all the rest of us!"

"Except I know what's coming."

"Not necessarily! You might be killed in a car crash, for all you know!"

Phillip's father burst out laughing. "I might," he said.

"Then, for God's sake, get something to do! Something for *all* of you to do. Get a little place where you can raise some pigs, someplace that needs a lot of fixing. You can't *be* yourself as long as you're just sitting around *thinking about* yourself."

"Well, yes and no," said Phillip's father. "Tell me, do you always . . . do this?"

"Not often enough," said Aunt Mil. To Phillip's astonishment, she seemed embarrassed. "If I've been rude—"

"Oh, no!" said Phillip's father politely. Her steely eyes sharpened on him for a second, in grim appreciation.

"I'd be glad to show you around," she said. "I'm something of a matchmaker between people and houses."

Phillip's father nodded cautiously. Already his mind seemed to be moving away from the conversation. His imagination had been captured, Phillip thought, and he was miles ahead.

"Well," said Aunt Mil, "a pleasure to meet you, Mr. Johnson. I've enjoyed getting to know your son." She turned toward the kitchen. Phillip and Kris hastily gave their attention to their tea. Aunt Mil's glittering eyes skimmed across them impersonally. "You'll come visit sometime when your wife is back?"

"Yes, we'd enjoy that." Phillip's father had risen to see his guest to the door. The oxygen cord slid off the carpet onto the kitchen linoleum, with a slight sound. Aunt Mil glanced at it and up at his face. He looked, as he had all morning, clear and vigorous and changed. Phillip could see that she liked him, and he was glad the two of them hadn't met till now.

When the door was opened, Thea stood on the step, her tail as erect as Aunt Mil's back. "Miaow," she said, clearly and courteously, looking straight into the eyes of the departing guests.

"Hello, Thea," said Aunt Mil. They passed each other, Kris followed, and the door closed.

"*Phew!*" said Phillip's father, pushing a hand through his hair. His eyes met Phillip's. "She goes for the throat!"

"They both do," said Phillip. His father's eyes sharpened on him curiously and then glanced away.

"You're braver than I was, at your age," he said, and moved to the table and sat down. Immediately Thea jumped into his lap and rubbed her face hard on his unshaven chin. "Hi, puss," he said. "Hi, puss."

Phillip glanced at the clock. It was one-thirty.

"Straighten up those . . . pillows, will you?" his father asked. Phillip did, retrieved the rest from the closet, and closed the door.

"You want some lunch?"

His father looked up, away from the beaming cat in his lap and away from his own thoughts. "What is there?" he asked.

Phillip opened the refrigerator door. He took out a plate of fried chicken, golden and dusted with pepper; a knuckle of leftover ham; plastic containers that held potato salad, studded with bits of home-cured bacon, macaroni salad, applesauce; most of a quiche, with crimped rings of onion on top; a bowl of fruit salad spiced with ginger, and yogurt to put on it; and a half gallon of milk. Consulting one of the lists, he said, "There's also cheese and bread for toasted cheese sandwiches and soup in the freezer."

"Oh," his father said, looking at the array.

"She, uh, she's coming back *today*, right?"

His father nodded. "This afternoon. That's what she said." He withdrew his gaze from the food, with some difficulty, and met Phillip's eyes.

"You want a toasted cheese sandwich?" Phillip asked, straight-faced.

"No, I . . . don't think that'll be necessary."

□   □   □

Slowly, through half the afternoon, they ate: a spoonful of salad, a sliver of ham; cold chicken torn off with their fingers a shred at a time and studded with far more salt than was probably good for them, sharing with

Thea. After a while, in the middle of pouring a glass of milk, his father sighed suddenly and said, "Wish I had a beer!"

Phillip got up and looked in the refrigerator. On the bottom shelf were two beers, the brand his father used to like. He probably hadn't had one since last corn planting, the last season he'd been able to work. Without a word he twisted off the cap and put the bottle in front of his father.

"Well, I'll be!" his father said, holding it up and looking at the label. He sighed again and raised the bottle to his lips, and hesitated, looking at Phillip. "You like beer?"

The question, out of nowhere, left Phillip blank and groping. Did he like beer? He was not of the legal age to drink it, but of course, it wasn't legal for him to skip school, either.

"Get a glass," his father said. "I can't drink the whole thing."

Phillip got one, and his father carefully measured out a third of the bottle and then tipped his head back for a long, thirsty swallow.

By shred and by spoonful they whittled at the edges of the food. They spoke only to ask for something or to Thea. Phillip's father looked around him, as if seeing the house he lived in for the first time. Occasionally he looked at Phillip, who then kept his eyes on the food.

Slowly the kitchen darkened. Phillip got up to turn on a light and make a cup of tea.

"I haven't been much of a father to you lately," his

father said, looking not at Phillip but into the mists of his own mind.

Phillip took a tea bag out of the box and carefully, neatly folded the waxed paper shut and closed the lid. "It's okay."

"No. It's hard. You figure . . . your kids'll be grown, before you have to face this. You'll be . . . wise, and strong. You'll . . . have it all figured out." Now his father looked at him, measuring. "How old are you?"

"Fifteen."

"I thought I knew everything, at fifteen. You feel that way?"

Phillip shook his head.

"Good. I can't—I can't put things back. I wish to Christ I could! I can't . . . give you what I want to. But . . . you want to move? Like she said, some little farm—" His father paused and coughed hard.

No, thought Phillip. That surprised him a little. He still felt like a stranger in this house. It obliged him to be neater and politer than was natural. But he didn't want to lose Kris, or soccer next fall, or the gray house. . . .

"Stay in this school district?"

"Yeah," said his father. After a pause: "Get your mother some . . . goddamned ducks."

□   □   □

She got home later than they were expecting. The food was still out when she let herself in the door, and guiltily Phillip started packing it away. Her eyes passed over the laden table indifferently. She might have counted each elbow of macaroni and weighed the ham before she left, in her anxiety, but now she had forgotten that.

"Leave the chicken out," she said. "I'll eat a piece—and the fruit salad." She slipped out of her coat with a tired sigh and kicked off her shoes.

"Drive okay?"

"Yes, Carl." She rubbed one hand over her face and stretched her shoulders, where driving always got to her, and then went over and hugged her husband. Phillip looked away. A hug was unusual at any time, and in recent months his father was most often in the armchair, inaccessible.

This hug went on, reminding him that it was *their* life screwed up here, as much as his. They were his parents. He came from them and was meant to outlive them. But they had chosen each other, for love and comfort, and now their plans were ruined.

He should melt away, he thought, into his own room. But the hug ended, and his mother looked at him.

"Hi," he said. "How's Carrie?"

"Just let me get rid of this coat and use the bathroom, and I'll tell you."

They settled in around the table. His mother took a leg of chicken.

"This is warm!"

"We been . . . pickin' on it all afternoon," her husband said.

"So how's Carrie?" Phillip asked again.

His mother sighed. "Oh, she's . . . okay, really. She's going to be okay in a while."

"Well, what *happened*?"

"Oh, he just left her a note, saying he thought it would be best if they stopped seeing each other. Out of a clear blue sky, apparently. And that night one of her friends overheard him at the student center, explaining to another girl how his former girlfriend just couldn't *be there* for him. What makes her mad, of course, is that that's all she *did* do, and he dumped her when she tried to make it work both ways."

"So she's mad," said Phillip's father. "Good."

"Yes. She doesn't want him back. But she wants—oh, she felt special, and needed, and loved. She wants to be loved right now."

"Tell her to come home!"

"She'll be home at Thanksgiving, Carl, but she can't get back before then. Vivian will help."

"How is Vivian?"

Phillip listened to his mother tell the news, thinking that the trip had changed her. Maybe it was just tiredness, but she seemed calmer, at once resigned and capable. He liked the way she left the crumbs and little daubs of food on the table and went into the living room with her husband, pushed a couple of pillows onto the floor, and put her feet up. Thea jumped onto her stomach.

"We had company this morning," his father began. He sat a little sideways in his chair to look at her. They were both changed.

And this conversation was for them. Phillip didn't belong in it. He slipped off to his own room, leaving the door ajar. Only a low murmur of voices reached him, an occasional cough.

It's okay, he thought. I'm a teenager. I'm not *supposed* to talk with my parents.

And it *was* okay. He had a tiny hurt feeling in his chest, though, and he was somewhat lonely. He thought of going out and walking up to the playground. Maybe Kris would be there.

But he was really too tired. He'd awakened at three this morning, and he felt as if the cold had gotten into his bones in a new way. It made him feel fuzzy all over and lazier than he was lonely. He took out his English paper again and sat looking at the sun sign.

"A ballad," the teacher had told them. An easy rhyme scheme. Tell a story. Phillip decided a factual account of this little symbol really wouldn't do. But he could see it on the back of some motorcyclist's jacket, instead of a Confederate flag, or as the banner of a brave knight's little band of men. Yes, a knight.

The knight battled for Beauty in Strange Forms and won the respect of all. Unfortunately his ladylove could not bring herself to be identified with a pennant of such lowly origins. The knight was at a crossroads—

Suddenly Phillip became aware of raised voices.

"I'd *like* to," his father was saying. "I'm not used to a . . . house where there's only . . . people to think about. I want . . . more going on. I want Phillip to . . . have a dog, if he wants, and you to have ducks. [Cough] I'd like . . . to have a sow, and . . . feed her mash, and scratch her back with the paddle. Free-graze her, like we used to. Raise piglets—" His voice had begun to hurry and grow faint, and now he coughed hard.

Phillip heard a pause that was full of consternation, and then his mother said, "Who *is* this woman?" Then the level of their voices subsided, and Phillip couldn't hear any more.

CHAPTER TWENTY

Monday the school hummed with excitement. Obnoxious people achieved new heights, and teachers came down on them with a crisp authority rare this late in the term. Paper airplanes and spitballs flew. Phillip remembered Thea that morning, racing around the frozen yard with her tail kinked, dashing two feet up a crab apple tree and clinging there, glaring at him wildly. Definitely the weather was about to change. He had felt it himself. He'd looked at his sneakers that morning and shivered and put on his leather work boots instead.

In English class the teacher's eye ran nervously down his ballad, flinching visibly from the sun symbol that decorated every third verse. Phillip remembered he was a suicide risk.

It was hard to know how to handle this. He felt shy and dropped his eyes whenever the teacher looked his way, with her gaze that was meant to pierce and measure. He felt like giggling. He considered the probable effect of melancholy expressions and bold, cheeky grins and in the end made no response to her at all. That was probably the worst thing he could do. "Withdrawn," she would write in red felt tip in his folder.

After English he attended history. He hadn't meant to, but as he was approaching the big doors, he caught Mr. Pilewski's eye. Instead of going outdoors, he merely looked at the sky for a moment and turned away.

"Going to snow?" Mr. Pilewski asked. Phillip shrugged. He thought he saw a look of compassion on Mr. Pilewski's face, a tolerance and an alertness. The man knew something. What?

He was late for history but was allowed to slide into a seat without remark. On Mr. Blackman's face, too, very briefly, was the look of concern. Phillip flushed and sat staring at his notebook, missing almost everything about the Articles of Confederation.

This would have to stop.

Obviously the word had gone out. Maybe there had even been some sort of conference about him. He was visible now, and being watched, not with the hostility he'd imagined but with compassion, which was much worse. He had to be normal again. He had to fit in, so they would stop looking at him.

The bell rang, and it was time for lunch. Phillip evaded Kris by visiting the bathroom and then slipped out the nearest unattended door.

The air was cold and wet, the day gray. The only brightness was the ground, covered with fallen leaves. When he stopped at the farm overlook, the sky seemed high and the wrinkled clouds absolutely still. Two crows flapped across, their wings heavy. It seemed to take them a long time to cross the farm basin.

With a shiver Phillip turned away, shrugging into his bandanna vest as he started up the hill.

Today the kittens were on the doorstep, huddled together against the side of the house. They looked up at him with wide, still eyes, too cold to play. Too cold to move. He picked them up, and like little frozen lizards, they lay still in the crook of his arm, until his warmth penetrated and they started to purr.

They were still okay. They were healthy. But what fun was he getting out of them? What fun were they getting out of kittenhood?

He sat on the step and held them for a while. Looking down at their faces, he noticed how one kitten always met his eyes, with a look of recognition, while the other only looked at its brother or out at the world. This was how he could tell them apart, and he knew that he already loved the one that looked at him and respected the other for its determined catness.

Not all alike, he thought to Dr. Franklin.

"Well, you guys must be hungry," he said. The kittens tensed in his arms. They were looking beyond him, listening hard. By the time he caught on and turned the way they were looking, he heard the crashes, too.

Someone running, leaping recklessly down the slope on the other side of the brook, lemon-colored shirt bright in the brown woods, pale hair lifted in the wind of running. Phillip was disoriented and distracted, as the independent kitten leaped out of his arms, spitting—but it was Kris, now splashing through the brook in her sneakers.

"*Quick!*" she gasped, no louder than a whisper. "They're coming!"

As Phillip gaped, she snatched up the kitten from the ground, closing it firmly in the strong cage of her hands.

"Who?"

"Peabody and Pilewski. *Hurry!*" She headed back across the brook and up the bare slope beyond. There was no cover, and Phillip followed dazedly, wondering how far they would have to run.

But partway up the hill a large tree had fallen, and Kris dropped out of sight behind it. Phillip found her flat on her back, gulping huge breaths of air and trying to still the squirming kitten. He dropped beside her and noticed for the first time that his own kitten was digging in its claws. Bright drops of blood beaded up on the backs of his hands.

"On the road," Kris said, when she had the breath to spare. "They should just about be here."

Several minutes passed. The kittens' ruffled feathers were smoothed, and Kris was breathing quietly, when

Phillip began to hear a rhythmic tramping on the road. It sounded incredibly loud and went on for some time before the two men appeared.

They seemed unsurprised to find a house here, walked clumsily and matter-of-factly down to the door, their shoes trampling the weeds and the patch of sand where the sun sign was. They pushed the door open without knocking and went inside.

Now Phillip began to hear voices. He couldn't make out what they were saying. In a moment Mr. Pilewski appeared in the back doorway, completely filling it. He looked keenly down the brook and up the slope, as alert and formidable as a Polish knight. Phillip disciplined his first reaction and did not duck, and evidently the top half of his head passed for a section of tree trunk. Mr. Pilewski turned back to the kitchen. "Nothing," he said.

Their voices went on inside for a moment more, and then both came out into the yard again. Mr. Peabody put his hands on his hips and stood looking around, seeming a trifle uncomfortable at such an expanse of space.

"I don't know where to start," he said.

Mr. Pilewski shook his head. "Not much point. Besides, it's deer season."

"Oh!" Mr. Peabody looked around nervously. "Isn't this land posted?"

"Not that I know of."

"So near the school—and I *know* that boy doesn't have an orange jacket!"

Mr. Pilewski shrugged. "Maybe. I don't think we know a goddamned thing about him. I'm not even sure he's been here."

"Well, the ax, all that wood—"

"Maybe somebody from the farm. Maybe a hunter."

"Oh." Mr. Peabody turned, frowning. One of the kittens suddenly let out a loud cry. Neither man seemed to notice. "Well, it was worth a try," Mr. Peabody said. "You didn't get anything from Madeline Rossi?"

Mr. Pilewski shook his head as they started up the slope through the weeds. "I just asked if he worked there, and she said he did. I think . . ." His words were muffled by distance.

Phillip rested his cheek against the log. He listened to their footsteps dying away and to the loud clamor of the brook. He felt a little sick, until Kris turned to him, her eyes bright with triumph.

"They don't know *anything*!" she said.

"They know I've been skipping."

"Not a big deal. This is *nothing*, compared with what some people get away with!"

But I'm not that kind of person, Phillip thought. "What will they do?"

"You'll get a couple warnings, but they definitely won't suspend you. Just say you had to get away and think—"

"Anyway," said Phillip, sitting up straight and letting the kitten go, "what are *you* doing here?"

She glanced away, watched the kittens prowl along the log. "I . . . followed you, Monday. Just to make sure—"

"Make sure *what*?"

She flushed. "Make sure you weren't doing drugs! Make sure you weren't gonna kill yourself!"

"Why did you think—"

"Oh, come *on*, Phillip! When people start acting weird, you *think* about it! I knew I'd feel like a jerk reading your obituary, so I found out! And I haven't followed you since, okay? I really couldn't care less what you do, especially if you don't want to tell me—"

She broke off and got to her feet. Phillip sat staring up at her, not knowing what to say.

"I have to get back," she said.

"Are you going to be in trouble?"

"No."

She looked tall and remote, closed off from him. A bad way to end the adventure. It *had* been an adventure, Phillip realized. He felt the triumph rising in him. So he'd been too stunned to enjoy it at the time. So what? Now it was there to think about.

"Hey," he said, stopping her as she turned. "Thanks. How did you know they were coming?"

"It was a *little* obvious, the way you snuck off—"

"It was?"

"Well, they were watching. And so was I. I saw them follow you."

"Shit." The sense of adventure rapidly paled. "Now what do I do?"

Kris hunkered down and picked up a twig, rustling it in the leaves to catch the kittens' attention. After a moment's thought she said, "It might work out. They never caught you. They'll want to find out what you're up to. So they'll watch, and if you don't come here for a while, they'll forget about it."

"Yeah, but . . ." He stopped, eyes on the kittens as they stalked the twig. Up here, away from the comparative shelter of the hollow, they seemed even smaller and more domestic.

"You'd have to do something soon anyway," Kris said. "It's getting so cold."

"Mmm." Phillip watched the pencil-point tails of the kittens. Barn cats get along okay, he was thinking, but a barn was more shelter than the gray house. Besides, when snow came, he would leave an unmistakable trail.

But he *liked* coming every day. It wasn't what he'd intended, it wasn't all the gray house meant to him, but he missed chores. Like his father, he needed something to do, something to care for. . . . He looked up at Kris, who was frowning at him, and he wished he had something simple and clear to say to her. She was on the verge of getting mad again, and he didn't know how to stop it—

"I can't take them," she said abruptly. "I figured I would, but now with this greyhound thing—" She was *not* angry, only gruff with embarrassed sympathy. None of us know a goddamned thing about one another, Mr. Pilewski. . . .

"Something'll work out," he said. "I haven't fed them yet. Want to come down and see?"

She looked down at the gray house, in all its beautiful loneliness, and shook her head; reluctantly, he thought.

She was shivering, and her nose was red. "No, I really have to get back. Are you coming?"

Phillip shook his head, smiling. "Can't face it. Tomorrow. I'll deal with it tomorrow."

"All right." She punched his arm lightly and turned away.

At the top of the slope she turned again. "What did you name them anyway? Bonnie and Clyde, or Frank and Jesse?"

Phillip gaped. She grinned and waved, and disappeared over the top of the ridge.

Monday. Chicken sandwich day. She must have had a hard time not laughing.

□   □   □

He collected the kittens and headed toward the house.

They had come here so directly. Was it a known place? Somewhere to smoke pot and make out?

That must be rare, Phillip thought. There was no graffiti scratched anywhere, no litter. Most people wouldn't come so far.

Big tracks crossed the patch of sand, which he had never stepped on. He thought the sun sign would be obliterated, but after a moment he found it between two footprints, intact. That made him feel a little better.

Inside nothing seemed to be touched, but the space felt invaded. It seemed shabby and dreary now since their eyes had looked at it: Mr. Peabody's kindly, piercing stare, the glittering blue-eyed gaze of Mr. Pilewski.

The kittens didn't notice. They were happy to eat. Phillip stood watching. He thought he should take them back now.

What stopped him was the thought of Dr. Rossi's eyes. They would look disappointed and saddened, because once again the kittens would be her problem.

Besides, it would be a pain carrying them.

Tomorrow, then. He would bring his bike. And between now and then he would have figured out what to do with them.

□   □   □

The sky was wrinkled like a washboard, high and still, and as Phillip crossed the cornfield, he felt like an ant: small, slow. He didn't like the feeling of the air, the chill, the sense almost of vibration.

The tiny pellets of snow had been falling for several minutes before he noticed them. At last one bounced off his coat sleeve, as he stuck out his thumb and a driver stopped for him.

□   □   □

Dry as sand, the snow collected against the curb outside the clinic in a half inch dune. Otherwise the pavement was bare. A searching wind had come up. Phillip hurried toward the side door.

A woman was going in ahead of him, with an old Labrador on a leash. The dog paused beside the dead marigolds and cocked its leg. Glancing down a second later, Phillip saw brilliant splashes of red across the faded browns and yellows. He frowned, feeling stupid. Hadn't the red faded out of the marigolds? There was red on the ground, too.

"Hello, Margaret," said Dr. Rossi at the door. Only Dr. Rossi's friends came in the side door and before office hours. The old Lab wagged his tail and trotted heavily inside. His owner let the leash drop and pointed to the red-splashed marigolds.

"I see," said Dr. Rossi.

"There's been a little blood in the past two days, but this is much worse." The woman's voice was firm and almost casual.

"Well, come inside, and I'll take a look. Oh, Phillip! Could you help me lift him?"

"Oh, Madeline," said the owner, "let's not. He hates the table!"

"All right," said Dr. Rossi. She knelt beside the old Lab, who wagged again and licked the air near her face. The owner held his collar, and Phillip stood by ready to help, watching Dr. Rossi do the examination.

It was almost a trance. She pressed the fingers of both hands around the rib cage and then almost up inside it, as if she could reach right into the dog and feel each organ. Watching, Phillip felt drawn into the trance as well. He didn't know what she felt with her hands, but he knew when the dog shifted away from her, when it tensed, and when it didn't care.

At last she stood up.

"It's the kidneys, of course. I could take an X ray—"

"Let's not," said Margaret. She looked at the dog, and Dr. Rossi looked at her. When Margaret looked up, Dr. Rossi's eyes slid away again.

"We know what to do," Margaret said. "Don't we?"

Dr. Rossi's eyes were stretched wide to hold back tears, but it wasn't entirely working. "Yes," she said, turning away for the needle.

"I knew when I came in, really. Oh, Thor—yes, what a good dog!" The Lab was panting in discomfort, but he still seemed cheerful and gave a wag at the sound of his name.

"Phillip, will you hold him?"

"I will," said Margaret quickly. She knelt and hugged the dog, pressed her cheek against his head, and whispered a few words. He wagged his tail slowly from side to side.

"All right," Margaret said. There were tears where her cheek had rested on his head, but she held him calmly, and calmly his body slackened. He was heavy, and he fell out of her arms and sprawled on the floor.

She stood up, with tears streaming down her face, and suddenly there was a small clatter as Dr. Rossi angrily threw down the syringe. She pulled Margaret into her arms, and Phillip, who had stayed only because Dr. Rossi seemed determined to need him, looked for an exit.

But he was in a corner, between a supply shelf and the table, and they were blocking the way. He made some slight move anyway, out of embarrassment, and fear at the prickling of his own eyes.

Without looking up, without a word, Dr. Rossi reached out and drew him in.

Into darkness and softness, sniffles and shaking breath, the smell of perfume and the smell of tears. His own tears started, but it was dark. No one could see. He put an arm around each of them, Margaret and Dr. Rossi, and they stood that way.

At last there came a cautious tap at the surgery door. "Dr. Rossi?" Sharon called. "Three-thirty."

Dr. Rossi stood back from the embrace with a loud sniff. "Five minutes, Sharon." Phillip turned away from them as they blew their noses and wiped their eyes. He rubbed his face on the sleeve of his jacket.

"Phillip, can you help Margaret carry him to her car? Use the side door."

"I'll do it," he said, stepping in Margaret's way before she could bend down. He gathered up the heavy dog and carried him outside. The wind was even sharper, the air full of snow.

Margaret opened the car door for him. He put the dog on the backseat, and pulled the old dog-smelling car blanket over him.

"Thank you," Margaret said.

Phillip looked away, feeling the cold wind acutely on his still-damp face. "Sorry," he said.

"I know." Margaret squeezed her eyes shut for a moment and then got in the car and drove away.

CHAPTER TWENTY-ONE

"**B**rr!" In the back room Dr. Franklin stamped snow off his boots. "It's damned *cold* out! Starting to add up, too."

Phillip looked past him out the door. The afternoon was darkening rapidly, but the parking lot was bright with snow.

"It's not supposed to keep on like this, is it?"

Dr. Franklin shrugged. "Doesn't look like stopping to me. About an inch out there now."

If there was an inch here, on warm pavement in the valley, how much more was there at the gray house?

Sharon poked her head through the door. "Phillip, phone for you. You want to take it out here? Press the flashing button."

"Hello?"

"Phillip? Hi." His mother. "It's so awful out—don't start home. I'll come pick you up as soon as my pie gets out of the oven."

"I was gonna call you," Phillip said. "I'm going to . . . Dave's house tonight." Out ahead of his words was a void. In fascination he listened to himself bridge it. "He asked me to . . . help him with some homework and have supper. I thought I'd stay overnight, so you wouldn't have to come get me."

Thin. It sounded thin to him and should have

sounded thin to her. But lately her instincts were blunted. "Well . . . all right," she said, expressing only generic parental caution.

"See you tomorrow," Phillip said, and hung up the phone. He glanced at Dr. Franklin, who was busy resupplying his black bag. But from Dr. Franklin's perspective the conversation must have seemed perfectly innocent. When he did look up at Phillip, it was with this encouraging thought.

"Maybe it'll snow so much they'll cancel school."

"Maybe," Phillip said.

□   □   □

"Give you a ride home, Phillip?" The last two people had canceled their appointments, and Dr. Rossi was in the hall, putting on her coat.

"No, that's okay."

"It's no *trouble*, Phillip," she said, a trifle sternly. A man was waiting for her, and Phillip was glad, though jealous. After a day like this she should have someone to go home with.

"No, it's all right."

Her beautiful eyes focused on him severely. "You are a very stubborn boy," she said, and swept by, brushing him with her perfume. Now he had made her angry. For some reason that pleased him slightly.

He put on his own coat and stepped outside. The snow swirled beneath the streetlights. There was enough to scuff through, enough to make tracks in. He started across the parking lot.

"Hey, Phil, didn't your ride show up?" Dr. Franklin,

at the wheel of his station wagon, pulled alongside and stopped, slewing sideways a couple of inches.

Shit! Phillip thought, but that was a waste of mental energy. He found himself with nothing to say and stood there, all too obviously groping for a lie.

"Oh," said Dr. Franklin. "So that was all a fabrication?" His eyes were bright and watchful. Snowflakes drifted through the open window and caught in his beard. Phillip decided to remain silent.

"Well . . . none of my business," said Dr. Franklin, unconvincingly. "But . . . need help?"

Jesus! Phillip thought. All of a sudden he was surrounded by people wanting to help him. *Insistent* on helping him. He started to shake his head and saw Dr. Franklin frown.

"Actually, yeah," he said. "Could you lend me five dollars, just till payday?"

Dr. Franklin wasn't giving up. He sat there looking up at Phillip with a kind of formidable openness. If not given a true answer, if turned from and run away from, he looked ready to leap from the car and tackle. *Christ!* thought Phillip. What had he done to make so many people notice him?

"I've got those kittens hidden out," he said. "I gotta go take care of them."

Dr. Franklin hissed his breath across his teeth, glancing at his snowy windshield and lashing wipers. "They have any shelter?"

"They're in an old house," Phillip said. "But I should get up there. Build a fire."

"Any chance I could drive you and take them home with me?"

They're *all right*! Phillip felt like shouting. I take *care* of them! He had never expected to feel guilty about saving the kittens' lives.

"There's no road," he said. "You couldn't get there."

Dr. Franklin's eyebrows and the end of his beard drew toward each other in a deep, worried frown. "Does anyone know about this? Does anyone know *where*—"

"Someone knows," said Phillip, with a rush of thankfulness to Kris.

Reluctantly Dr. Franklin relaxed.

"Is five dollars going to do it? Make it ten—and here, take my car blanket. You're planning to stay out there, I understand? You should have a hat. Here. Your head is just like a wick, you know. Think of yourself as a candle: Your head is the flame, burning off all your body heat." The hat came from the backseat, like the blanket, and carried a strong scent of cow manure. "Are you all set?"

Phillip nodded.

"Good! You're in for a goddamned uncomfortable night, Johnson!" Dr. Franklin thrust his mittened hand out the window and shook Phillip's hand. "Good luck—Christ, kid, don't you have any *mittens*?"

"No." Phillip thrust his hands in his pockets and backed away.

Dr. Franklin shook his head. "All right, but I meant it. I'll take 'em if I have to." He rolled up his window and, spinning slightly, drove away.

□ □ □

Phillip went across the road into the grocery store and bought cheese and a chocolate bar and a very small flashlight. The store was packed with people, stocking up as if for a major blizzard and complaining excitedly.

When he went outside again, the weather seemed to have grown even more miserable. The snow in the air was magnified by headlights and streetlights, slushed and splashed by cars. As Phillip trudged up the road, wearing the blanket over his shoulders, he thought with unusual affection of his home. Pie, his mother had mentioned . . .

"Need a ride?" Three people stopped to ask tonight. The first storm of the season made a solitary walker with a blanket on his shoulders look especially pathetic. Phillip said no each time. It was good to walk. The wind, the blurred lights, the steady rhythm of his own feet seemed to smooth everything out in his head. Weather he could handle.

Beyond the rim of the suburbanized world the sky was dark and full of snowflakes. The road was white, his own tracks black and wobbly behind him.

The farther he went, the smarter people seemed. They had gotten home already or not gone out in the first place. Phillip passed houses where the light shone yellow and hospitable out the windows, where families could be seen at supper, where the snow had stopped melting off the car hoods and was beginning to mount up. He passed mailboxes with little caps of snow and horses in roadside pastures, surprised-looking, wearing snow blankets.

He walked slowly. His work boots had little tread left, and he slid backward with every step. For so long he had been light on his feet, his sneakers pushing the frozen ground back behind him easily. Now winter dragged on him like ankle weights. It was a long, cold, uphill walk.

At the farm the barn was dark, with a deep blanket of snow shouldering the sky. A wide river of tracks, human and dog, led toward the yellow house. Its lights seemed kind and homey, but far away, like a Victorian Christmas card. They'd left the cows in, safe from the storm. Phillip could hear hay rustling and an occasional soft moo. The bulk-tank motor droned in the milk house.

Out across the white expanse of cornfield, the wind swirled in all directions, as if uncertain what to do next. Soon, Phillip thought, the snow would stop. Then it would get even colder.

□　□　□

Tonight the locust trees seemed very black and wild, and the gray house looked cozy, wearing a coverlet of snow. Phillip trudged down through the weeds, stumbling a little as his feet missed the familiar path. He looked back at his own tracks, like the wallowings of a moose. Now no one who passed could imagine this place deserted.

Inside he knelt at the fireplace, standing the little flashlight on its end to illuminate the widest possible area. He would light a fire first and then look for the kittens.

But as he dragged the first stick out of the kindling pile, something moved in the back of the fireplace. Phillip's heart thumped. He grabbed the flashlight and pointed it, and the kittens blinked at him. They were curled in a tight ball, behind the heap of ashes against the back wall. Perhaps they remembered the earlier fire and were trying to find its warmth.

He picked them up. They were reluctant to move or break apart from each other, like someone in bed on a cold morning, not wanting to stir the covers.

"Just a minute, guys," he muttered, settling them in their box. At the loosening of his clenched jaw, his teeth began to chatter.

Quickly he broke the sticks, laid a fire, and touched a match to the dry kindling in several places. It seemed to take forever for the separate points of flame to catch and grow and unite into a single bright young blaze. Then it took another forever for the blaze to deepen and begin to give back some heat.

Phillip set a pan of water on the flames and crouched close. The kittens huddled beside him. Occasionally one gave a convulsive shiver.

Phillip didn't take them on his lap. His jeans were soaked. The knees, only inches from the fire, steamed and scalded him. The wet fringe of Dr. Franklin's car blanket began to smolder. He pressed his foot on the smoking place.

Now the water was close to boiling. He made his cocoa, stirred it with a twig, wrapped his hands around it.

Just so his father had wrapped his hands around a coffee mug, in the corner of the couch Saturday morning.

One kitten yawned and stretched, spreading its toes at the fire. The other trilled and curled on its back, exposing its belly to the heat. Phillip wanted to touch the fluffy tummy, but when he started to reach, he found his hands didn't really want to move. He sat staring at them. Big red hands. His father's hands.

"You look so much like your father." People like aunts and cousins, people who didn't know him well enough to think he looked like Phillip, used to say that to him.

Someday soon all he would have left of his father was what he could see in a mirror.

The tears flowed easily. He felt no inner convulsing, no difficulty. For a few moments he was interested by this. He imagined firelight glinting on the water that trickled down his face.

Then he heard a small drip. Startled, he looked down and saw that his tears had reached the floor. Suddenly it wasn't easy anymore. He remembered what he was doing: crying for his father, who was going to die.

He loved his father.

He had to put the cocoa down because the difficult, harsh crying was making it slop on the hearth. Now he could press his palms against his eyes and bow his head down to his knees. He could smother his sobs against his wet jeans, hug himself, curl himself as small as possible. His face was hot, salty, stinging. He didn't know what would ever make him stop.

At last something stung his leg: a kitten, sharpening

its claws. It met his eyes with a warm, chummy look, pleased with itself and sure of pleasing, swarmed up onto his knee, and butted its head against his nose. A few more tears fell on its soft fur. It curled in the crook of his arm, blinking up at him and purring.

He put another stick on the fire and watched the flames, watched the breath of the kitten slow to sleep. The same thoughts that had sent a hot gush of tears down his face and tied a knot in his breath a few moments ago, now presented themselves simply for him to look at.

He loved his father.

It was possible that he'd never thought this before. There had been no need. It would have been like saying he loved air or his metabolism. And lately whatever had been on his frozen mind, it wasn't love.

Now image after image came: his father condemning the duck pillows; standing in the garage door with the oxygen cord trailing down the steps; facing Aunt Mil, that smile at the corner of his mouth; holding up a bottle of beer and saying softly, "Well, I'll be!"

His father had become visible again, changed, full of a weary, beaten grace. He was resigned and angry, sad and full of humor. Phillip realized how much he had been missing his father. How much he *would* miss him.

"Shit." He was crying again, so helplessly it was like bleeding. Once he had feared cutting himself, alone up here, or being shot. This was the real hemorrhage. Really—as real as the hearth, as real as the fire, as real as the storm outside—his father would die.

Everyone will die.

His father would die too soon. He was sick now and soon would die.

But he's doing *better*! His attitude—

He would die anyway. His attitude could not change that.

It was like a rock wall in Phillip's mind that every straying, hopeful thought ran up against. It had been there a long time, but he'd kept turning his back on it. Now he was helpless—almost worse than helpless, almost running into it on purpose, turning back to it whenever he strayed off a little and found relief. He will die. Die. Die.

Never see him again. Never get to ask him things. Never get to show him, with your life, what you learned from him, where the two of you differ.

Hemorrhage.

But it couldn't last forever. Phillip began to feel dehydrated, and his tears dried up. He couldn't stop shivering.

After a while he thought of the hot cocoa, reached down for it.

It was stone cold.

Knowing how long he must have been crying forced a few more tears—concentrated, stinging and itching on his cheeks. He got up and went outside.

The snow had stopped. He was surprised to see only a couple of inches on the ground and bright stars tangled in the locust branches. For a long time he leaned against the door frame, weak and drained. Very slowly, the clean, bright beauty of the night made its impression on him, striking deeper and deeper until it seemed to be everything. He didn't move. He hardly turned his eyes; but he felt them widen and widen, and each long breath seemed to draw the smell of the snow to the very center of his chest. He felt clean and blank and open, as if the black wind of the universe roared without impediment through his heart.

He was getting very cold.

Finally he was too cold. He bent and scooped up two handfuls of snow from beside the step and pressed them to his hot eyes and cheeks. Then, with snow water trickling down his face, he went back inside, stoked the fire, and made more cocoa.

□　　□　　□

Eventually, as the windows were beginning to show gray with the dawn, he ran out of wood. The fire sank and died, and the stone chimney began to cool.

Slowly the room became visible. The woodpile was gone. The kittens' box was empty. The ax, the hatchet, the jar of matches, the cat food pans and the blackened saucepan he'd heated his water in, elements that had made this a primitive home, seemed only lonely, separate articles in the gray light. He and the kittens, huddled at the cooling hearth, were no longer residents, but only waiting to leave.

Stiffly Phillip stood up and began to festoon himself with possessions: ax, hatchet, cup and blackened pan, strung on his belt; Dr. Franklin's huge flannel shirt over his jacket; the blanket on his shoulders. Finally he turned to the kittens.

"All right, little dudes." It was the first he'd spoken

in hours, and he had to clear his throat. "Time to go."

Clanking slightly, he stooped to pick them up and tucked them inside his jacket, buttoning it around them. He walked to the door, paused with his hand on the latch, and looked back.

His meager domestic arrangements were swept away, and with them, the sense of being at home. Phillip felt his original excitement rise again at the bareness and loneliness of the place.

It was known to other people. He didn't care. That made it real and made caution imperative. It would be awhile before he came back, but he would come.

He went out, closed the door, and walked up through the weeds to the road.

CHAPTER TWENTY-TWO

t was a beautiful morning. The sun was just up, the sky a deep and brilliant blue. Snow sparkled in little rainbow prisms, cascaded off wind-stirred branches, drifted glittering in the air. The brook ran black beside the road, and snow mounded the rocks and banks, beautiful and soft. Blue jays flashed and screamed in the trees. Crows cawed heavily; chickadees chickadeed and hopped and pecked. Despite his encumbrances and his boots, Phillip felt light. Very light—starving. And lighthearted, and empty-headed.

In the cornfield sun gleamed on the golden stubble, which just showed above the snow, and on the weeds in the margins and the silver gray fence posts. An apple tree caught his eye. It stood at the edge of the field, leafless but covered with beautiful golden apples, like a tree from a fairy tale.

In the farmyard he heard milking machines and a radio behind the steamy barn windows. The woman, bundled up and wearing a blue ski hat, came to the door as he was passing. "Hi!" called Phillip, and waved. Her eyes were wide and amazed, but she waved back automatically.

His wave and voice had disturbed the kittens. First one head and then the other popped out the opening of his coat. He looked down, and they looked up, as wide-eyed and amazed as the woman at the barn door.

"*Mewp!*"

"It's okay," he said, putting up his hands to catch them.

But the kittens had never seen a wide white world like this. One buried its head in Phillip's coat again. The other held his gaze desperately and cried. Phillip stroked the stripes between its ears with one finger, and it stayed out looking at him till he reached the road and the first car passed.

The road had been plowed and well driven on. It sparkled black and wet in the sunshine, and the cars sent up little splashes as they passed. Once an empty school bus rattled by. Phillip looked at the sun and tried to estimate what time it was. Past schooltime surely. Long past breakfast.

The kittens began to squirm, still unwilling to look at the world but no longer comfortable. Phillip felt their legs pushing his stomach, one climbing on the other's head. Cries, plaintive or annoyed, came from under his coat. He was glad to see the fringes of settlement at last. Soon he was at the corner of his own street and, with only slight hesitation, turning.

The driveway was already shoveled—scraped bare, actually, down to the dark wet pavement—and the mailbox was cleared. The flag was up, but his mother had left the cap of snow on top. Phillip could see where her fingers had brushed it, putting up the flag. The edges of the snow were starting to trickle and drip in the sunshine.

As he got closer, he could smell coffee and apples and spice. He hoisted a slipping kitten, climbed the steps.

He could see his father at the table, a newspaper spread open to the real estate section. His mother was pouring herself a cup of coffee. As Phillip clicked the latch of the storm door, she looked up and gave a start that slopped coffee across the counter. His father looked, too, and both seemed to freeze in disbelief and incomprehension. Phillip pushed open the door and came inside.

"Phillip," his mother said. Slowly she set her cup down on the counter, reached for a towel, and dried her hand. "Phillip, what . . . it's nine-thirty. Why aren't you in school?"

Phillip stopped on the mat, so snow couldn't melt from his boots onto the clean floor. He couldn't think what to do next, not even which boot to take off first, or how to do it, or whether instead to unbutton his jacket, let alone what to say and which parent to address. His mother, having asked her question from pure reflex, was staring at him wide-eyed, openmouthed. His father was more composed, more alert and formidable. Of course, he was better prepared, having some slight inkling of strange comings and goings. Phillip saw him recognize the ax and hatchet.

Abruptly the frozen moment cracked. A kitten lost hold of Phillip's sweater and dropped halfway down his body before it caught again, dangling there with all but its head showing. The other kitten popped out the top of his jacket, looked around, and wailed.

His mother's eyes bulged, his father started and smiled, and there was a thump down the hall in one of the bedrooms. Almost before the sound had registered on their ears Thea was among them, arched and bristling, yellow eyes ablaze. She stalked toward Phillip and sniffed the lashing tail of the lower kitten, swelled even larger, drawing in a breath that seemed as if it would never end, and hissed.

Both kittens shot upward, and their claws found flesh. Phillip yelped, and Thea lowered her tail and ran.

"Oh, my goodness," his mother said faintly, drew in a breath, and asked, with a great deal more firmness, "Phillip, what on *earth* is going on?"

Phillip detached a kitten from his shoulder, with a sound like Velcro, and handed it to her. The other was crawling around somewhere near his armpit. He reached in to find it. "I . . . had them hidden. Out in the woods. They were going to be put to sleep."

"Well, for *heaven's* sake, why couldn't you bring them home?"

It was a stunning question. Why not? He knew there was a reason: a feeling that he couldn't make any demands or add extra complications, a feeling that this house had to be kept bare and sterile, like a hospital. But that feeling was dissolving so fast that he could hardly grab hold of it and name it to himself.

"Here," his father said, reaching up for the kitten she held. The one Phillip had was the one that looked away from you, and this one looked straight into his father's eyes. Phillip's father looked back, with the expression of delight and discovery that Phillip always remembered. It seemed very young, almost as young as the kitten's own wide gaze. Tenderly, with the hand that bore the broad wedding ring, Carl Johnson cupped the kitten against his chest.

"How long have you had them?" his mother was asking.

"About a week." The one he held squirmed and cried, and he had to put it down. At the corner of the hallway he saw Thea's long white whiskers, pointing intently.

"Where have you been keeping them? How did you feed them?" And here it came. "Have you been skipping school to do this?"

"I . . . cut a few classes."

"You cut a few classes! How many classes?"

"Um . . . quite a few."

"Phillip Johnson, for goodness' sake! Does the school know about this? Why hasn't anyone called me?"

"I don't know," he answered. He wanted to forget the school; he wanted it to forget him. And he wanted that piece of apple pie warming in the toaster oven and filling the kitchen with its aroma. Then he wanted another, and after that, a shower, and his warm bed. . . .

"Well, what should I *do?*" his mother asked as Phillip began to pry off his wet boots and divest himself of equipment. "Should I *call* somebody? Are you going to do it *again?* Can I *trust* you, or do I have to take you to school every day and pick you up? I never dreamed—oh, my goodness gracious, *look* at that pot!"

Meanwhile, the independent kitten was stalking across the linoleum, shoulders ominously high and tail like a bottle brush. It sniffed Thea's dish and backed away, catching her scent.

Breathing hard and momentarily stumped for words, his mother reached for her coffee. Phillip could hear the kitten in his father's hands start to purr.

The one on the floor neared the table. It saw the oxygen cord, stopped, stared, and commenced a wary, circling advance. Phillip saw his father's free hand slowly reach down. Suddenly he tweaked the cord.

Phzzzt! The kitten exploded, Thea growled and ran, and Phillip's father burst out laughing.